*The Right Dog for Joe*

# Books by Irmengarde Eberle

THE RIGHT DOG FOR JOE

A CIRCUS OF OUR OWN

FAMOUS INVENTORS FOR YOUNG PEOPLE

LISTEN TO THE MOCKINGBIRD

THE STEAM SHOVEL FAMILY

TOO MANY SHOES AND STOCKINGS

A GOOD HOUSE FOR A MOUSE

THE VISITING JIMPSONS

THE VERY GOOD NEIGHBORS

HOP, SKIP AND FLY

A FAMILY TO RAISE

SPICE OF THE WIND

BASKETFUL

# The Right
# Dog for Joe

by

## IRMENGARDE EBERLE

*Illustrated by Jean Macdonald Porter*

jEb37r

Dodd, Mead & Company
NEW YORK

PRINTED IN THE UNITED STATES OF AMERICA
BY THE VAIL-BALLOU PRESS, INC., BINGHAMTON, N. Y.

# Contents

U. S. 700913

# *Illustrations*

*The Right Dog for Joe*

CHAPTER ONE

# *Vacation Time Is Coming*

EVERYBODY in the house was busy this Saturday. Joe's new stray dog was busy barking on the screened back porch. Mrs. Collins was using the vacuum cleaner in Dr. Collins' study. And Joe and Marty were working upstairs in the spare bedroom.

Joe was on the small stepladder which was parked in the closet doorway. He was taking hat and suit boxes

1

down from the shelves so that they could be cleaned out. His sister Marty stood below him and took the boxes from him.

"Housecleaning!" Joe exclaimed impatiently. It was a bright morning in early June and he had other uses for such days. "I ought to take Patch out for a run," he said to Marty. "Listen to that dog bark. And he'll go right on, too, till I take him."

Marty said, "He's lonely out there on the porch."

Patch had been with the Collinses for about two weeks. Joe had found him by the service station, looking lost and scared, and had brought him home to keep until he could find someone who would take him.

"We can't stop to play with old Patch now," Marty went on. "We've got this closet to finish." She groaned. "It does seem to me that Mother is having us do more cleaning than usual."

Marty was a year and a half older than Joe who had recently turned twelve. And she talked almost like a grown-up now, Joe thought, just a little precise and posey.

"I wish you'd go on being just a kid, Marty," Joe said to her. "I like you best when you talk just like me and the other kids."

Marty laughed. "I talk the right way for my age," she said and set down the hat boxes Joe handed her. "But all this cleaning and putting things in order . . . I think something's going to happen around here. Maybe Dad's going to take that government job he and Mom were talking about last month, and we're going to have to move or something."

"Maybe that's it," Joe agreed, thinking it over.

"Mom would want to have everything in the house just right if we're going to sub-let it," Marty said.

"I wish Dad would stay here and go on teaching at the University, the way he does now," Joe said. "I like it here. I don't want to move."

Then he and Marty went on discussing the fact that their father was a physicist and knew a lot about atomic energy. It would be important, if the government wanted him, and a thing to be proud of, they knew. And it might be really interesting to go to a faraway place where atomic energy was being produced.

"We'd see a lot of new things," Joe said. He handed Marty another large suit box and told her, "That's all."

"All right," Marty said. "I'll give you the dustcloth now so you can wipe off that shelf."

From Canfield Road, which ran past their house, came the sound of boys' familiar voices and of dogs barking.

"Hey!" said Joe. He stuck his head out of the closet, listened alertly, then quickly climbed down from the stepladder and rushed to the window. He looked eastward.

And there coming up the road were his friends, Dan,

## The Right Dog for Joe

Phil and Jim and their dogs—Dan's Betsy, a Manchester terrier and beagle crossbreed, and Jim's English setter, Pal.

Joe called to them, "Hi, Dan, Phil, Jim! Hi, Betsy and Pal!" The boys shouted back; and the dogs raced across the lawn, stopped below Joe's window and pranced around and gave low barks as Joe talked to them. All dogs liked Joe, especially those who knew him so well.

"Come on down, Joe," Dan called. "We're going out to the Jasons' farm!"

"I can't," Joe called back. "I have to help around here a while longer."

The dogs, Betsy and Pal, had gone around to the back of the house to sniff at Patch through the screen door. An occasional short bark came from there as the sniffing and wagging conversation went on between the three.

"Gee, I wish I could go with you," Joe said.

To console Joe, Phil explained that they were not going to stay out at the Jasons' long today, anyway.

Jim too said, "We're coming back right after lunch— about two o'clock maybe."

Dan called Betsy and Jim whistled to his dog.

"Good-bye," Dan said to Joe. "We've got to go."

"Good-bye," and "Be seeing you," said the others.

The two dogs raced back to join their masters and the small party went on westward.

Joe watched them go. Then his eyes looked beyond

4

*There coming up the road were his friends*

them, following the road as it cut through a broad
meadow and, a half mile farther on, curved in between
high-wooded hills. These were the Brewster Hills after
which the town was named. The road disappeared from
sight between them. Beyond, one could see range upon
range of higher mountains, with long, gradually rising
slopes. Some were bright green, others, shadowed by
passing clouds, were darker; and very far away they
were all blue with distance.

Joe thought of where the boys were going. The Jasons
lived on a little farm up in the broad valley, just beyond

6

the nearby hills. The Jason children, Tom, Charlotte and Ellen, had a hound called Rambler that Joe had given them. Rambler was another of the stray dogs Joe had befriended in recent years and given away. Joe wished again that he was going out there now, with his friends, to see the Jasons and old Rambler.

He left the window abruptly and turned to his sister. She was sitting before her mother's dressing table, gazing at herself in the mirror. She was holding her hair back, this way and that way, to see how it looked best and paying no attention to the big smudge of dust on her left cheek. Nor did Joe notice it more than in passing, for he was pretty dusty himself from that work on the top shelf of the closet. Besides, he, too, had other things on his mind.

"Marty," he said, "we ought to have a dog again—a dog of our own to keep."

"I know," Marty agreed. "We really need a dog, now that we haven't old Jolly anymore."

Jolly was their police dog who had died of old age a few months before.

"Sure," Joe declared. "I'd like to keep Patch but Dad and Mom want me to give him away."

"Patch isn't much to look at," Marty said. "But he's nice."

Mother's voice came up the stair well. "Marty! Joe! Do go on with your work or you'll never get through."

"Okay, Mom," Joe called out. He seized the dustcloth, climbed back on the short stepladder and set to work. But he went on talking to Marty, who had started dusting the boxes.

Joe told Marty, "I guess it's because we might move if Dad goes to that atomic energy job that he and Mom don't want me to get a new dog to keep just now."

And Marty agreed. "After all," she said, "if it's a teaching job, we might move to a big city and live in an apartment house where they don't even allow dogs."

Joe said, "Yes, I guess that's what Mom and Dad are thinking about."

He was through dusting the closet now and, with Marty's help, he stacked the suit and hat boxes back up on the shelves. Then he climbed down and said, "Let's get going," and dashed into the hall.

Marty followed more leisurely, washed her hands in the bathroom and then went into her own room to make her bed.

Joe ran downstairs. He was a rather lean boy, of an average height for his age. His ash blond hair was beginning to show signs that it would some day be much darker, perhaps as dark as his mother's; and his eyes were a keen blue, like his professor father's. He was in a hurry because Patch was still barking and needed his company and because he had some more things to do for his mother.

8

Joe went out to the back porch and let Patch into the house. The dog jumped up at him happily and Joe took his front paws in his hands and said, "Hey! Old Patch! Good fellow, Patch!"

Patch was a mixture of a number of breeds. He was a little larger than a wire-haired terrier, was tan and short-haired and had a very good tail for wagging. A large white spot covered one side of his head, like a cap that had slipped down over his right eye and ear. He had a funny expression on his face and sometimes almost looked as though he were laughing.

"You want to come in and be with the rest of us for a while?" Joe asked. Patch wagged joyfully and followed Joe as he turned and went back through the kitchen and on to the study where his mother was.

"Mom," Joe said, leaning in the doorway of the study, "I sure wish I could have gone out to the Jasons' with Phil and Dan and Jim and Betsy and Pal."

His mother, a small, brisk woman, looked at him with bright, laughing eyes and said, "You can go next Saturday, Joe."

Joe then thought of what he and Marty had been discussing upstairs. "Why are we housecleaning so 'specially hard? Is it because of the government job? Is Dad going to take it and move us away from here?"

Mrs. Collins answered, "That's not certain. We won't know about that for some months yet. Our extra thorough

9

housecleaning of closets and shelves and bookshelves —all that is in preparation for what may happen this summer. I want to get the hardest part of the housework over with early."

Then, of course, Joe must know what it was that was in the air for this summer. And Marty, hearing part of the conversation, came and sat on the steps, halfway down, to listen too.

Mother switched off her vacuum cleaner and said, "Well, it's about a trip your father and I may take, children. There's a conference of scientists in Paris in July, a little over a month from now. Your father may be one of the men sent over from the United States."

"Dad must be terribly brilliant," Marty said, "to get asked for that."

"He sure is, I guess," Joe put in. "First the government wants him for atomic energy business and now he may get sent to this conference, too!"

Marty asked, "Mother, did you say you would go along?"

"I certainly will," said Mother. "I wouldn't miss a chance to go to Paris for anything. I've only been there once and that was fifteen years ago, when your father and I were on our wedding trip."

Suddenly another side of the matter came into Joe's mind. "But Mom," he asked, "if you go away, where would Marty and I stay?"

Mrs. Collins explained that they would stay right here at the house and their Aunt Edna would come and look after them.

Marty was delighted. "Oh, I love Aunt Edna!" she cried. "She's so nice."

Joe frowned. "But she doesn't like dogs," he said.

"That's right," said Mother. "And it's one of the reasons why Dad and I wish you would find a home for Patch quickly, so that in case we go to Paris . . ."

"Oh," Joe said. He could see that he certainly would have to get poor little Patch out of the way now. That an otherwise nice lady like his aunt could actually dislike dogs was just one of those things he could not understand. But that's how it was. Father was bad enough about dogs, Joe thought. He was indifferent to them. But Aunt Edna really disliked them. That was terrible!

Mother started the vacuum cleaner again and went on about her work.

Joe leaned against the door jamb and wondered whether he should mention again that he wished the family's plans were settled, so that he could get a dog of his own for keeps. But he decided not to. It might tire Mother to hear that and tiring people never got you anywhere.

Mother advised, "And now you'd better get those blankets and hang them out to air, Joe. Hustle a bit, if you want to be free this afternoon."

11

## The Right Dog for Joe

"Okay, Mom," said Joe.

He started from the room, rubbing Patch behind the ears. Someone was coming up the front walk and Joe turned to see who it was. It was Mrs. Carney, Phil's mother. She was carrying a strawberry cream pie on a plate. It made Joe's mouth water.

He called out, "Hello!" and then, "Mom, Mrs. Carney is here!"

Mrs. Collins answered that she would be there in just a minute. And Joe ran and opened the door for their visitor.

Mrs. Carney was a plump woman, as firm as a white turnip fresh from the garden. She was energetic and almost always busy. Joe held the door for her, just as his mother came forward.

"Hello, Frances," Mrs. Collins greeted Mrs. Carney. Then, seeing the pie, "Oh, how wonderful that looks!"

"I just made an extra one for you while I was making one for us," Mrs. Carney said, matter-of-factly. "I'm practicing up on my baking, as I'm going to make some pies and cakes for the church bazaar next month."

"We'll have it for supper tonight," Mrs. Collins said, taking the plate in both hands and admiring it. "What with all this housecleaning, I haven't done any baking for ages. And Dr. Collins does love pies and cakes."

"So do I," declared Joe.

Mrs. Carney laughed. "Of course, the pie is partly

12

for you, too, Joe."

Marty came running down the stairs. She didn't like to be left out of anything that went on.

"Yum," she said, gazing at the pie.

Mrs. Carney and Mother, talking about the Church bazaar which was to be held the first of July, settled themselves in the living room. Joe and Marty hung around, waiting for something of special interest to them to be said.

Mrs. Carney, who was a widow, owned a large, rambling summer boarding house called Sky Inn. It was up in the mountains, seventy miles or so north of the town of Brewster Hills. She started to tell Mrs. Collins she would be going up there next week to start getting it ready for the summer. It was the first of June now and Mrs. Carney wanted to have the place open for early guests by the fifteenth.

"I'll be back and forth between here and there until school closes and Phil can come up to the Inn with me," she said.

Joe began to listen to the talk more intently because he loved Sky Inn. He had been up there for a while last summer as the special guest of his pal, Phil. Mrs. Carney had told Joe when he left that he could come up again for two weeks the following summer. Joe was just a little afraid she might have forgotten.

But Mrs. Carney had not. Her very next words to

13

Mrs. Collins were, "By the way, you must be sure to send Joe up for a couple of weeks again. Phil likes to have him; and Joe is really quite useful around the place."

A broad smile lit Joe's face. He waited intently, eager for his mother's reply.

"Why, that's lovely," said Mrs. Collins. "Of course, he may go."

Joe gave a jubilant yip and asked quickly, "When can I come?"

So they settled the date for that. He was to come up the end of the second week in July. Joe felt that summer was really on the way at last, for now the most important and the best part of his vacation was planned.

"I'll go over and see Phil this afternoon, as soon as he gets back from Jasons' farm," he said to his mother and Mrs. Carney, "and we'll talk about Sky Inn."

Then he went out on the front steps and jumped off into the grass and yelled, "Whoopee!" And Patch caught the excitement and leaped about and barked. Joe said to himself that there just wasn't any nicer place to go than Sky Inn. It would even make up for not having a permanent dog till the family's plans were settled for next winter.

CHAPTER TWO

## *A Home for Patch?*

IN THE early afternoon Joe came out of the house with Patch and looked about him cheerfully. Mother had said she would not need his help any more today, so he could go to the Carneys and see if Phil had returned from the

Jasons' farm yet.

He started down the walk with Patch pulling on the leash. But he stopped to look northwestward over the mountains, for it was in that direction that he would go when the time came for his visit to the Carneys' Inn this summer. He took a deep breath and gazed on in happy anticipation.

Then he heard his father inside the house, saying good-bye to his mother. Dad had been home for lunch but was going right back to the University where he had been all morning. He had no classes on Saturdays and, anyway, the spring term was over for him. University professors and students certainly got a good break, Joe thought, for their vacations started weeks earlier than public school vacations. Dad was going to do some more laboratory work of his own today, just because he liked to. Besides, he had said, he had to consult with the president of the University about some special matters. Joe wished his Dad was not quite so busy, so he could stay at home more.

As Joe waited, Dr. Collins came out of the house and Joe called, "Hi, Dad!"

Dr. Collins smiled at him. "Are you and Patch coming my way?" he asked. "I'm going to the University on the bus, as your mother wants the car."

He was a stocky man, with thick, dark, slightly graying hair. His eyes had that contented but lively look that

16

people have who are very much interested in their work. He looked particularly pleased just now.

"Yes, we're going that way," Joe said. "I want to talk to Phil about this summer."

"Nice of Mrs. Carney to ask you up to the Inn," Dr. Carney said.

"It sure is!" Joe exclaimed.

They left the path together and turned east on Canfield Road. Now they walked in sunlight, now in the cool shadow of the tall, old oak and elm trees. Patch trotted ahead of them, pulling on his leash a little, his head and tail held high.

Dr. Collins watched the dog and, for the first time since Patch had been staying at the house, actually chuckled at him. "What a dog," he said.

Joe seized upon this opportunity to try once more to arouse his father's interest in the dog a little.

"Did you ever notice that Patch sometimes looks as though he's laughing?" he asked. "He's really a funny dog."

"A comedian?" asked Dr. Collins with a brief smile. But in a moment Joe could see that the dog had slipped out of his mind again. He was too absorbed in thoughts of his own.

They passed a few people on the sidewalk and Patch barked loudly each time.

"He's very noisy," said Dr. Collins.

17

"No barking, Patch," Joe said firmly. But Patch barked again as the next person came near.

"*Sh-h*," Joe told him. "Stop barking." He turned to his father. "I'll teach him to be quiet. He'll learn soon. He's smart." It was most unfortunate that Patch had to behave so badly just now when they were with Dad.

Dr. Collins smiled and shook his head doubtfully at Patch. "Find him a home, Joe," Dr. Collins said.

"Okay," said Joe a little dolefully.

"And Joe," Dr. Collins went on, "I wish you wouldn't pick up any more strays for a while. We've got enough to attend to without that in the next few months."

Joe said, "I don't think there'll be any more around for a while, Dad. There aren't usually so many stray dogs. It just happens once in a long time, usually."

They came to the place where Elm Street ran into Canfield Road. Dr. Collins would catch the bus here for the University, which was a mile or so farther along. They parted and each went his own way.

Joe walked south. His father certainly did not like dogs as much as he did, he thought. But he really had always been pretty nice about him and the strays he collected. He would surprise Dad with what he would do this afternoon. He would attend to Patch's future even before going to Phil's to talk Sky Inn. He thought of the two other stray dogs he had befriended and how easily he had found good homes for them with the Jasons

18

and the Applebys. He could surely do as well for Patch.

And how would he start planning for Patch? Well, actually, he had known someone all along who wanted him and that was Mary Lou Denis. She was a few years younger than he, but went to his school. She always stopped and petted Patch when she saw him, and once she had said that she wished he were hers. Well, why not? Joe would go to her house right away and ask her.

He walked along briskly, pausing only long enough, from time to time, to pick up a handful of small stones to throw at tree trunks. He always aimed at a knothole or other spot and tried to make a direct hit. But just the "plunk" of the stones hitting the bark was a pleasant sound.

He followed a street curving up a slight hill. And there, a little way ahead, he saw a group of boys and girls he knew, with their bicycles. Mary Lou was riding on Dick Jones' handle bars.

He called to her. Dick brought his bicycle to a stop close beside Joe and Mary Lou slid off.

"Hello, Joe!" she cried. "And here's little Patch!" And she knelt down and petted the dog. He waggled joyously and stuck his nose up at her face, giving her a quick wet lick.

Joe said, "Mary Lou, once you said you'd like to have Patch. Well, if you want him, you'd better take him now.

19

## The Right Dog for Joe

My father and mother say I have to give him away soon."

"Of course, I'll take him," Mary Lou said. Then she added quickly, "If my mother will let me."

Joe said they had better go and ask her mother right away. So they set out together, leaving the rest of the crowd with the bicycles.

Mary Lou took Patch's leash and led the way. She certainly did like that dog. Joe smiled. This was going fine. He was fixing things up easily for Patch. Reaching Mary Lou's home, which stood at the end of the block, they raced across the lawn but slowed down as they came to the doorstep of the red brick house. Mary Lou opened the door and she and Patch and Joe went in.

"Mommie!" Mary Lou called. "Mommie! I want to ask you something. And please don't say no."

Mrs. Denis' voice reached them from the kitchen. "How can I promise that before I know what you're going to ask me?" she called back, laughingly.

The children passed through the living room which was spotlessly clean and pretty. There were rose-colored window curtains and a vase of many colored flowers stood on a low table. They came to a stop in the kitchen doorway. Patch squeezed between their legs and cocked his friendly, eager head up at Mrs. Denis.

Mary Lou's mother, a short, plump lady, raised her hands that were as pudgy as old-fashioned pin cushions,

"Why, what a funny-looking, cute little dog you have
there, Joe," she said

and she smiled.

"Why, what a funny-looking, cute little dog you have there, Joe," she said.

Mary Lou, happy at this cheerful opening, explained how Joe had found this stray dog and that he was going to give him to her.

"Oh dear, no!" exclaimed Mrs. Denis. "I've never cared so very much for dogs and I really don't want the responsibility of one. Besides, there's our cat, Mike. The dog wouldn't get along with our cat."

Mary Lou sat down and took Patch on her lap. He sniffed her hair and tried to lick her face. "Oh, he would get along with Mike," she said. "Please let me have Patch, Mommie. Look how much he likes me."

Joe said, "Patch does like Mary Lou better than anyone. And he'd make a good watchdog for your whole family, Mrs. Denis."

"No, don't beg me. I won't have a dog. We've never had a dog and I'd just rather not," she insisted.

There was a sharp "*Fsst!*" behind them and Joe and Mary Lou looked around and saw Mike, Mary Lou's small yellow, white and brown tomcat. He had his back arched and his tail straight up in anger and fright at seeing the dog. In another second Mike darted at Patch and slapped him soundly. Then he sprang away across the living room and Patch followed him like a shot out of a gun.

Joe yelled at Patch to stop but the dog had no thoughts for anyone but Mike. The cat scampered across the davenport and Patch, leaping up toward him, bumped against the vase of flowers standing on the low table. It toppled to the floor, and water, flowers and broken glass made a devastated area of the living room.

Mrs. Denis rushed into the room. She cried, "For goodness' sake, children, get that dog out of here!"

Joe and Mary Lou were already doing their best to stop the dog-and-cat battle. Joe grabbed for the dog and, after several tries, finally got a firm hold on him. Mary Lou opened the front screen door and the cat slipped out to safety.

Quiet descended on the room—a quiet too tense for comfort.

"Well!" said Mrs. Denis then, "now I guess you can see why you can't have a dog, Mary Lou."

Joe and Mary Lou were crestfallen. Joe said in a low, small voice, "We'll clean this up, Mrs. Denis."

"We'll do it right away," promised Mary Lou and hurried out of the room. In a moment she was back with a broom and dustpan, a bucket to dump the glass in and a mop with which to sop up the water.

Mrs. Denis was trying hard not to lose her temper. Joe could see that. There were two little places at the corners of her mouth that twitched and her jaws were firmly set. Now she turned and went back into the

23

kitchen. "All right," she said in a resigned tone. "Do the best you can with that floor. And don't say anything to me about dogs again, ever."

Joe took Patch into a corner and said, "Sit down," in a gentle but very positive voice. And the dog obeyed. Poor Patch, Joe thought, he just didn't know any better than to chase cats. He had no idea how much trouble he had made for himself and for Joe and Mary Lou. But he did know something was wrong and was quite subdued. He stayed in his corner while Joe and Mary Lou cleaned up. Finally, when Joe was ready to leave, the dog went with him, holding his head and tail low. He knew he was still in disfavor.

Mary Lou stood and watched them go. Then she ran after them and called Patch and petted him. She had tears in her eyes. "Oh, goodness, if only that hadn't happened!" she said. And after a pause added, "Look, Joe, I wish you wouldn't give this dog away to someone else yet. Please wait a few days. Maybe something will happen to make Mommie change her mind."

Joe was amazed at her. He had no such hope. Mrs. Denis had been much too angry to leave any such ideas in his mind. But he was sorry for Mary Lou and for Patch, too. To make her feel better he said, "Okay. I'll wait a while. But I can't wait too long because of my Dad."

She thanked him. Joe tugged at Patch's leash and he and the dog got started on their way. Joe did some serious thinking as he walked along. Was there any-thing he could do to make Mrs. Denis forgive Patch? He shook his head at his own question. He couldn't think of a thing.

To make himself feel better, he went around to see Phil now, as he had intended to do all along. But Phil was not at home.

"He came back from the Jasons' farm about two," Mrs. Carney said, "but now he's gone off somewhere else again."

"Oh, I'll look for him later," Joe said. He thought he'd better take Patch to his own screened back porch before he got into any more trouble.

When Joe came up the walk of his home, the living room was bursting with sound, for Marty and a girl friend were playing a new record and singing.

But Marty, seeing him come in, called out, "Oh, Joe, Dad just called up and said it's all settled—he and Mother are actually going to France the middle of July."

Joe felt excited. It was interesting to have your parents going to Europe. But still it was even nicer to have them just stay at home. Aunt Edna's coming was a certainty now which made it definitely necessary to find Patch a home quickly. If only Patch and that nice cat, Mike, had not made all that trouble at Mary Lou's house.

## CHAPTER THREE

# *It Gets Around*

Over Sunday, Joe and Phil finally got together and made plans about what they would do at Sky Inn during the summer. And this was still going on when they walked home from school together Monday afternoon. They were talking about what fishing tackle they could take to the mountains. They had plans for fishing all the streams for miles around when Joe came to the Inn in July.

"I sure wish you were coming up with me right away when school is out," Phil said. And Joe answered that he certainly did, too.

Phil was staying at the Applebys, now that his mother had gone up to the Inn. He wanted Joe to come over and take a look at his room but Joe said he couldn't. He had asked Mary Lou to come to his house that afternoon, for he had something to tell her. He, at last, had an idea about what they could do to win her mother's liking for Patch.

When Joe reached home he found that his mother and father were both out and Marty was reading her teen-aged magazine in the living room. He went into the kitchen and got himself a jelly sandwich and a glass of milk.

He ate and drank in quiet enjoyment while Patch looked on, his mouth watering. For once, Joe didn't give him a single bite. That had to do with this plan he had in mind. It was hard, though, because Patch loved bread and jelly above all else. He sat tense and almost trembled with eagerness every time Joe took a bite.

"Just a minute," Joe told Patch. "Your time's coming. Wait."

Then, looking out of the kitchen window, Joe saw Mary Lou coming along by the back way, so he took the half slice of bread and jelly he had laid aside and went out with Patch to meet her.

27

"Hello, Joe," she said. "Tell me the idea you have. Will you, please, quick?"

"Well," he explained, "it's like this." He sat down in the grass, so she did, too. And he went on, "I thought that if we taught Patch some tricks, your mother might see how nice he is."

Mary Lou was delighted with the idea. "One of the things we have to teach Patch is to be friends with cats," she said.

"Yes, I guess that's pretty important," Joe said, remembering what had happened at her house.

And Mary Lou added, "We'll start with kittens because kittens aren't afraid of dogs, so it will be easier to train him with them."

Joe complimented her on that thought. But while they were deciding from where they could borrow the kitten to practice with, he said they might as well start teaching Patch his first trick.

He held up the dog's front paws and said, "Sit up, Patch." After repeating this several times, he gave him a tiny bite of the bread and jelly he had saved. Then he and Mary Lou took turns making Patch sit up and each time they rewarded him with a bite to eat. They grew so interested in this that for a while they forgot about the kitten they had to borrow.

Patch couldn't figure out just why Joe and Mary Lou wanted him to sit up but he was willing to do it with their help, since it pleased them so much.

In between times he would race around them and bark, and then come back to them to see what they wanted him to do next. Both Mary Lou and the dog were so enthusiastic that Joe had great hopes.

Things were really going fine, he thought contentedly. Almost anybody would want Patch with tricks. And wouldn't Joe's father and mother be pleased when he got his last stray dog placed in this way.

"Patch is smart," Joe said to Mary Lou. "He'll learn sitting up in no time. And then we'll teach him some other tricks. He might even be as good as a circus dog if we just keep at him."

"I'll teach him to bring in the newspaper, once I get him home," Mary Lou said. "Mommie and Daddy will like that."

The back screen door of the house opened and shut and Marty came out, calling "Joe! Telephone for you!" And she went back in.

"All right," Joe answered. "I'm coming." He scrambled up from the grass and ran toward the back door. Patch started after him, then thought better of it and sat down and looked at Mary Lou happily. She put one arm around him and gave him a hug.

She called after Joe, "Hurry back! We have to teach Patch some more tricks!"

"Be back in a minute," he cried. "Keep an eye on

29

Patch. Don't let him wander off. He's just beginning to feel at home here."

Joe hurried on and in another moment he was sprawling on the chair by the telephone.

"Hello," he said into the instrument. "This is Joe."

"I'm Jim Parker," an unfamiliar voice came over the wire. "You don't know me but I've heard of you. I understand that you're the boy that takes care of stray dogs in this town."

"Well, yes. Only I think that just now my father doesn't very much want me to . . ." Joe began.

But Mr. Parker went right on. "I'm down here at my grocery store on Warren Street, near the bridge across the Wallford Brook. I thought you'd want to know that there's a lost dog down here."

"Yes?" Joe said in quick response.

"No collar, no license," Mr. Parker went on. "And he looks scared. I hear you took care of that stray near the service station last month."

"Yes, that was Patch," Joe said.

"Want to see what you can do for this fellow?" Mr. Parker asked.

"Sure," said Joe. "How'll I find him? What kind of a dog is he?" He just had to help a lost dog. Probably his father would feel that way, too. What his father had said about not taking in any more dogs was the kind of thing people say when no stray dogs happen to be around at

30

the moment.

Mr. Parker was describing the dog as probably a mixture of a small poodle and a Scotty. "You can't miss him, he looks so miserable and lonely."

"I'll come right down and get him," Joe promised. "Please try not to let him run away."

"Don't know if I can coax him to stay around here," Mr. Parker said. "I threw him a couple of dog biscuits but he's too scared to take them."

Joe told Mr. Parker he would be there as fast as he could, and put down the receiver.

Marty called from the living room. "That isn't about

31

another stray dog, is it, Joe?"

Joe admitted that it was.

His sister came out to the hall where the phone was. She said, "Dad and Mother won't like your getting him a bit—not just now when Aunt Edna's coming. And besides, we still have Patch."

"I know. But I'll give this new dog away today or tomorrow. Then I guess it'll be all right," Joe said.

Marty asked, "But how did this man who phoned ever happen to know about you and dogs?"

"I don't know," said Joe, running one hand through his hair and thinking the matter over. "I guess it just gets around."

Mary Lou came in from the back yard with Patch. The pink ribbon that held her straight dark hair back was dangling at the very end of one strand. Her pink face was shiny. "Come on, Joe. Let's work on more tricks," she said.

"No, I can't anymore now," Joe said.

"What happened?" she asked. "Are you going somewhere, Joe?"

"Yes, I have to see Mr. Parker about a new dog," he explained.

Joe went to the hall closet to get some things he needed. From a hook he took the smallest of several dog collars and a leash. He also took some tiny dog biscuits, the kind dogs get for dessert, and put them into one of his pockets.

Then he went to the front door with a quick, "Good-bye. Be seeing you."

"Oh gosh!" exclaimed Mary Lou. "Now I'll have to try to teach Patch by myself."

"I'll help you," Marty offered.

Joe was pleased. He liked it when any member of his family wanted to help him with one of his dogs. He gave her a broad smile. "Thanks, Marty," he said and then hurried away.

He went along Canfield Road for a quarter of a mile. Flowers bloomed in the yards of the scattered houses he passed and the smell of these and of green plants and damp earth was on the wind.

Some girls he knew were playing on the Applebys' lawn and there, too, was Teddy, the big boxer he had given these neighbors in the winter. Teddy was sniffing excitedly around a tree trunk near the girls. Probably smelled a squirrel.

Joe called out to the girls and they called back. The boxer had raised his head instantly at the sound of Joe's voice and now came bounding to him. Joe stopped to whack him fondly.

The dog's strong, muscular body grew taut with delight. Teddy never would forget him, Joe knew, for taking care of him when he was lost and nobody seemed to want him. The boxer would always be his friend. Joe

33

could not stop long just now, for he had other work to do. And he could not let Teddy come with him either. He had to tell him to go back and Teddy, after a little hesitation, obeyed.

Joe hurried on faster now, for the sake of the new lost dog. He kept his eyes open for him, just in case he had run this way.

He thought, "I'm certainly going to be busy if I have to find this new dog a home, too. I sure hope Dad and Mother won't mind if I have to keep him a few days."

He turned south and again east, following the street that curved along the brook. A gray light lay over the town. Joe looked up and saw that a great thunderhead had formed and had hidden the sun. He hoped it would not rain before he caught the dog. He came into Warren Street and could see Parker's grocery store a block ahead. Now he began to look for the lost dog in earnest.

His eyes searched the side streets and the grassy places along the brook but there was no sign of the dog. Coming to Jim Parker's store, he looked in through the plate glass window. And beyond the display of oranges and canned goods and soap and cereals, he saw a large, heavy man with a red face waiting on a lady.

Joe went inside and asked him, "Are you Mr. Parker? I'm Joe Collins."

"Oh, hello, Joe," Jim Parker said. He was wearing a large white apron and it made him look like a snow-

34

covered mountain. He excused himself from his customer and came from behind the counter and stuck his head out the door.

"I've been trying to keep my eye on that dog," he said, "but it's hard to do when you're busy like I am. He stayed here quite a while, trotting up one side of the street and down the other, hunting for somebody. The last I saw of him he was running down that way." He pointed north. **U. S. 700913**

"Thanks," said Joe. "I'll see if I can find him." And he hurried on.

The street he turned into at the corner dipped sharply downhill so that all the houses had a slanting base line. A little farther on, and to the left, there was an empty lot overgrown with weeds and grass. He walked slowly, so as not to frighten the dog, should he come upon him.

He arrived at the vacant lot and there, just a few feet away, among the sparse, straggly weeds, sat a small, scared-looking dog. She was short-legged and chunky, somewhat like a Scotty. Her white and gray coat was half straight and half fluffy, as though she were partly poodle, too, just as Mr. Parker had described. Her ears were pricked up to tense points. Before her lay a battered, dirty felt hat and the dog had her front feet on the brim.

Joe could see that she treasured it. She probably thought she was guarding it until her master should

35

return. He wondered what kind of a man would give his dog a hat to guard and then desert him. How cruel and mean a man must be, he thought, to do that to a dog.

The dog was watching Joe, fear and longing in her sad eyes. He began to talk to her, his voice friendly. He sat down in the weeds to let the dog get used to him. After a while he took some of the small biscuits out of his pocket and threw one on the brim of the hat. The dog jumped up in alarm, then hungrily sniffed the biscuit and ate it.

Now Joe held one out to her. She came a little closer but her whole body was tense with uncertainty. She was too afraid to take the food. Joe tossed the biscuit to her and again the dog jumped back at the gesture. But in another moment she came and picked up the morsel again. She was very hungry, Joe could see that. She might not have eaten for days.

"It tastes wonderful to her," he thought with pleasure. Thunder rumbled and Joe looked up and saw that the sky was growing darker and more threatening. If only the rain would hold off. Rain would make things harder for him and the little dog. He kept on talking to her, trying to gain her confidence.

More than an hour passed and, fortunately, the rain had not come yet. It was evening and the sun, lower in the west, cast an eerie light from under the edge of the clouds. But things were going well between Joe and the dog, at last. He could pat her now. And he had thought of a name for her. "Shaggy," he said. "That's a good name for you." The way he said it made her feel better. She laid her head on the ground, stretching it out toward him in longing for love and safety.

A few minutes more and Joe was able to put the collar and leash on her. Then he held the dog away on one side of him and picked up the dirty felt hat. She growled fiercely, wanting to protect it.

"It's okay," he told her and gave her the hat. She took it in her mouth and held it firmly. "Okay," he repeated soothingly. "You can keep it. Nobody wants it but you. Come on now. We've got to go home."

37

She tugged at the leash, then came along somewhat gingerly, her tail and head held low, wondering what was going to happen to her. She walked along but every once in a while she stopped entirely and he had to talk her into coming farther.

He arrived at the grocery store, finally, and showed Mr. Parker that he had the dog. And Mr. Parker warmly expressed his satisfaction.

Joe was sorry that there was no one else in the store. He told Mr. Parker, "I wish you'd ask some of your customers, when they come in again, if they want a pet dog. My father won't let me keep extra dogs very long—maybe not at all anymore. So I have to find a home for this one right away. Maybe one of your customers might want her."

"Sure, I'll try to help you place her," said Mr. Parker. "And, by the way, you'll need some dog food. I'll give you a half dozen cans to take home with you, if you'll lug them. That'll be my contribution."

This would make things easier, Joe knew, for one of his mother's objections to his dog-collecting had been the matter of the high cost of dog food.

He waited outside with the trembling dog while Mr. Parker put the cans of food into a small carton and brought them out to him. Then Mr. Parker thanked him for coming for the dog and Joe thanked Mr. Parker for the food again. He went off with the loop of Shaggy's

*Joe thought, "Let it rain. I can't hurry with this dog"*

leash slipped over one arm and the cans under the other.

"Better hurry home," Mr. Parker called after him. "It's going to rain any minute now."

Joe thought, "Let it rain. I can't hurry with this dog." And he let the weather drift out of his mind. He had other things to think about. He was feeling more and more troubled about what his parents would say when he brought this new stray dog home.

Besides, he was having more and more difficulty getting the little dog to walk along with him. She was so frightened. She did not know where Joe was taking her and there was no way Joe could explain.

A few large drops of rain began to fall. They struck Joe sharply like light, cold pebbles and they made a noisy splattering sound on the sidewalk and on the leaves of the trees. The rainstorm was here.

If only Joe had not had the box of cans with him, he could have carried the dog and then he would have been able to make much better progress. He realized now that he should have left the cans behind and made a special trip down for them later. But he was already too far on his way to do anything about that now.

Shaggy kept pulling back tremblingly. It was hard going and the dog was pitiful. Joe put down his box, sat on the curb and took the dog in his lap. She quieted a little. But when he tried to go on, she pulled back again, unwilling to come.

40

Finally he took the dog under his free arm. And so, balanced on left and right by dog and dog food, he managed to walk a little faster, even though it was an awkward load.

He reached Canfield Road and there, some distance away, he saw two girls and a tan dog hurrying toward the shelter of a porch. They were Marty, Mary Lou and Patch. Patch was leaping about and barking at something that Mary Lou had. She was holding it way up over her shoulder and Joe could just see that it was a kitten. Well, that was good. The training of Patch had been going right on while he was away. They were trying to get Patch used to cats.

He did not call to them but hurried on, for the rain came down with a rush now. His shirt was soaked through to his skin in half a minute and the little dog's shaggy coat was plastered to her, making her look even more pathetic than before.

Joe's arms ached from the double load of dog and food cans. But he kept on and at last he reached home.

He had hoped his parents might not be around, so that he could break the news about this second stray dog gradually. But luck was not with him. They were both in the living room when he ran in at the front door and was out of the rain at last. His father was reading the newspaper and his mother was sewing.

Mother saw him first and she gave an alarmed gasp.

41

## The Right Dog for Joe

"Joe! Not another stray dog!"

Dad jumped up and took off his reading glasses and came into the hall. He stared at Joe and the dog in amazement. "No," he said. "No, I don't believe it!"

Joe, feeling apologetic toward his parents but loyal to the dog, said hesitantly, "It's just a little one. And you weren't here to ask."

His mother burst out in laughter at that. But his father frowned and looked as thundery as the sky outside.

He said, "Look, Joe, I just asked you to get rid of Patch and to stop collecting dogs. And here you come right on home with another stray!"

"But, Dad, I didn't think you meant . . ." he began and then went on, "I'm not going to keep either of them more than a few days. I just want to see that they're taken care of."

Dr. Collins said, "Son, the town is equipped to deal with such problems. It's not incumbent on us alone, in all Brewster Hills, to take care of homeless animals. And this is the last stray animal we are going to take in this year. That's really final."

"All right," said Joe, "I'm sorry about this new dog, Dad. But Mr. Parker asked me to come and get him. And . . ."

Just then Marty came dashing in with Patch, both of them very wet, too. There was already a lot of rain water

42

on rug and floor where Joe and Shaggy had dripped and now Patch shook himself vigorously, spattering more water about. And he barked at the new dog.

Over this noise Marty cried, "Oh, Joe, what a cute new dog you've got!"

Mrs. Collins exclaimed, "Oh dear, what a mess your dogs are making of the hall!"

Shaggy was trembling. She sensed that Patch had prior rights here and feared he might chase her away. But Patch was not unfriendly. He just barked out of a spirit of welcome and out of the gusto of his nature.

"What a racket!" groaned Dr. Collins and withdrew to the living room.

He sat down again and picked up his paper. It's all to the good to be kind to animals," he said. "But one has to keep such impulses under control, Joe."

"Yes, sir," said Joe. "But Dad . . ." And then he stopped. There was no use trying to explain because his father just did not feel about dogs as he did. He was interested in entirely different things. Still, he, Joe, was really in the wrong today.

Joe was sad because he had made his father angry. He was torn between loyalty to dogs and longing to be on friendlier terms with his father. But now he must put his mind on Shaggy.

"Marty," he cried, "please keep Patch here a while,

till I get Shaggy fixed up."

"Sure," Marty said and held on to Patch.

Joe went on through to the back of the house and put Shaggy on the screened porch. There he dropped her old felt hat and then dried her with a piece of clean white cloth he had found in a kitchen drawer. The dog was still trembling but she licked his hands, too. He was good to her and she trusted him more and more.

Joe opened one of the cans of dog food and gave her some in a saucer. She ate it quickly and hungrily. Then she picked up her old hat with her mouth, dragged it to a corner and lay down beside it.

"You'll be all right now, Shaggy," he comforted her. "Won't you?"

Joe thought to himself, "If I had left Shaggy out there, she would have been picked up by the dogcatcher. Then she would have been killed after a while because almost no one ever goes to the dog pound to take one of the lost dogs home." Surely Dad wouldn't want this dog to be killed like that."

What would Joe do if he heard of another lost dog in town? It was deeply troubling to think about that.

"But if I keep on picking up lost dogs when Dad asks me not to, he won't like me so well," Joe thought, "and it probably won't make him like dogs any better either."

He made up his mind he would not take any more lost dogs in for a while at least under any circumstances.

44

Meanwhile, he would make things better with his Dad, too, by finding a home for the new dog in the next day or so and by trying his best to get Patch fixed up with Mary Lou.

CHAPTER FOUR

# *A Workable Plan*

THE rain had stopped by the time supper was over. And when Marty and Joe had finished doing the dishes, they went outdoors.

"I'll get Patch," Marty said, looking up at the clearing sky. "And let's go look for another cat for him to associate with."

"Where's the kitten you and Mary Lou had this afternoon?" Joe wanted to know. Marty explained that she had been scared of Patch. They could not use her again.

"But Patch just has to learn to associate with other cats," she insisted.

Joe was pleased with Marty's enthusiasm over teaching Patch manners. It was going to save Joe a lot of work if she kept at it. He said, "You look for a cat for Patch, Marty, and I'll attend to Shaggy. I'll see if I can't find someone who'll take her off my hands right tonight . . . on account of Dad. I've got a swell idea. I'm going to try those new people, the Healys—the people that moved into the house on Elm street."

Marty and Joe went around to the back of their own house now. Patch greeted them noisily. But Shaggy lay still in her corner with her front paws on the dirty old felt hat she owned.

"Shaggy'll be all right by tomorrow, I bet," Joe said. "Patch will help her get playful and start having fun."

They put Patch's harness on and set off. First Marty held the leash a while and then Joe. Just before they got to the Healys they passed the Morrisons. And there, on the front walk close up to the street, sat the big black Morrison cat."

"Look!" said Marty.

"Good," Joe cried. "Now we can get to work with cat practice."

The cat was not afraid of Patch. She stayed right where

she was and looked the dog over calmly. But Patch leaped about, pulling on his leash with all his might, and trying to get at the cat.

Joe and Marty told him to quiet down. Joe held him and petted him and Marty went over to the cat and petted her, to show Patch that all creatures should be friendly with each other. And the dog finally stopped his prancing and sat down. But he still trembled with excitement and eagerness to chase the cat. It was going to be a long slow job to get Patch to learn to leave cats alone, Joe could see.

He had other business in mind, however, and now he told Marty that he thought they had better go on. So they started for the Healys, and the big cat looked almost sorry to see them go.

Mr. and Mrs. Healy were sitting in chairs out on the lawn. Joe and Marty could see them there as they crossed the street toward them.

"This is luck," Marty said. "It'll be easy to get started talking dogs with them out here."

Just then, Patch slipped his leash. Joe grabbed to catch it, but the dog was out of reach in a second. He went dashing and yapping happily across the lawn and up to the Healys. Mr. Healy jumped up angrily. "Get away from here," he said sharply to the dog. He bent down and picked up a stone from the flower border and threw it at Patch. The stone struck one of his hind legs and Patch let out a yelp, put his tail between his legs and ran back to Joe and Marty limping a little.

Joe grabbed his leash and held him by his side. "Hey," he cried angrily to Mr. Healy. "What did you do that for? Patch wasn't doing anything wrong. He wasn't hurting anything."

"Just keep that dog off my place," Mr. Healy said in a sharp voice. "Get him away from here." He was a thin gray man, with a narrow, firmly-set mouth.

"Gee," said Marty, "a real dog-hater. We better clear out."

Joe was so angry he could hardly think what to do. "To hit a dog with a stone and for nothing!" he murmured, stroking Patch who was more surprised than hurt. "And we were thinking of offering him little Shaggy! Come on. Let's go."

They hurried on past the house, turned a couple of corners and went home by the back way. Patch came along quietly, apparently subdued by his experience.

Mrs. Collins was in the back yard, looking at the pink and white flox at the far edge of the lawn. Joe and Marty told her how Mr. Healy had struck Patch with a rock.

"Why, that's a shame," said Mrs. Collins. "But why did you go over there at all?"

Joe explained. He said that the Healys were about the only people in the neighborhood he had not yet asked at some time in the past years whether they wanted one of his dogs. Mrs. Collins agreed that anything had been worth trying, as Dr. Collins had a good deal of reason to be angry with Joe for collecting this second stray. A home must certainly be found for her soon.

"Do go on trying tomorrow, Joe," she said.

Joe promised that he would and they all went indoors, Joe and Marty to do a little more of their homework, and Mrs. Collins to join Dr. Collins in the living room.

For the next few days Joe asked somebody every day whether they would give Shaggy a home. And as to Patch, Joe still hoped to be able to win Mrs. Denis over to take him for Mary Lou when the dog had learned several good tricks. But still Joe made some other inquiries for him, too, just in case that failed.

Mostly, he worked on Shaggy's problem, though. He even took her back to Mr. Parker's grocery store and showed him how calm and cheerful the little dog was now. And asked Mr. Parker again to try to help him place her. And Mr. Parker said he would.

So Joe sat down on a box, holding Shaggy in his lap, and every time someone came in to buy groceries, Mr. Parker told them about the dog's need for a home. And everyone was nice about Shaggy and talked to her or tried to pet her. But no one took her.

Finally Joe gave up and went home.

"I'll keep trying," Mr. Parker said, as Joe went out the door.

50

But Joe knew that, though Mr. Parker meant well, he was very busy and would probably forget about Shaggy much of the time.

He still thought it could not be too hard to place so nice a little dog. And so the next afternoon he set out right after school and went to a new part of town, where he had not yet offered a dog to anyone. This, he felt, might work better.

Eventually, he found himself away over on Melnor Avenue. He stopped in front of a red brick house and looked it over. It was well kept and seemed a good place for a dog to live.

He walked up the path and rang the doorbell. Footsteps approached and then a solid-looking, middle-aged lady, with curlers still in on one side of her hair, appeared at the door.

"What is it?" she asked Joe, a little impatiently.

"I just want to ask you something," Joe said hurriedly. "I want to ask if you would like to have a little dog. A mixed one but a very friendly, nice little dog."

"No," said the lady. "Thank you very much but we have a dog, a Pomeranian. She wouldn't allow another dog in the house."

"Oh."

Joe turned and walked on. He kept going from house to house, up one street and down another. He asked the same question of many men, women and children, inside and outside their houses. He did not run into another dog-hater, like Mr. Healy, but he just did not find quite the interest in his dogs that he was looking for. Some people, like the lady he had asked first, already had dogs. Others just flatly said "No," and that was that. Some led Joe on to talk about his dogs and listened interestedly. But, in the end, nothing came of all this. Nobody wanted Shaggy or let himself be put on the waiting list for Patch.

Joe was getting a little discouraged. He really had thought it was going to be easy to place, at least, Shaggy. But it wasn't at all. He was not having any such luck as he had had in placing the hound, Rambler, or the boxer, Teddy, in other months and years. And his father, of whom Joe was so very fond, was still angry with him about the whole dog business. It worried Joe greatly.

Hesitating before ringing another doorbell, Joe's thoughts turned to his own friends. There was Phil. Why couldn't Phil take Shaggy? He didn't have a dog at all and that never had seemed right. But Joe knew perfectly well that neither Phil, or his mother, really cared about having a dog. Strange, Joe thought, when Phil was such a nice fellow in every other way and such a good friend of his. He gave up the idea of trying to get the Carneys to take Shaggy. There was no use wasting time over it.

Joe had left Shaggy and Patch at home. They were out on the screened back porch, as usual, because Dr. Collins did not like them all over the house. The two dogs got

52

along fine together now. Shaggy was no longer afraid of Patch and romped with him joyfully. Really, Shaggy was not afraid of anything anymore. She had even given up her dirty, old felt hat which had comforted her so much at the beginning.

Joe wondered now whether he should have brought the dogs with him. Maybe it would have been easier then to get someone to fall for the charming looks or personality of one of them. But he had remembered what a poor impression Patch had made for himself chasing the cat, Mike, at the Denises and about the way Mr. Healy had chased him off with a stone. And to avoid anything so troublesome happening again, had chosen to come without them.

Joe had walked about three-quarters of a mile by now. He could see the Methodist Church, which his family attended, a little farther on.

He had come to a street corner, when a man's voice behind him said, "Hello there, Joe!"

Joe turned around and saw that it was the minister, Mr. West.

"What brings you all the way over here on a weekday, Joe?" Mr. West asked.

Joe explained what he was doing and how poor the results were. "Nobody seems to want a dog," he said in the end. "But dogs have to live."

The minister frowned. "That's right," he said. "Your

53

dogs need homes. I wish I could help you."

"Oh, thank you," said Joe. "I certainly need some help fixing things for Patch and Shaggy."

They started to cross the street but just then a huge truck came along and they waited until it had thundered past. In that moment, Joe had a wonderful idea. His face lit up with pleasure.

"Mr. West," he asked, "could I bring Patch and Shaggy to the church bazaar? Maybe have a little show with them doing tricks?"

Mr. West looked at him solemnly, thinking this over. Then he chuckled. "Why not?" he said. "Why, maybe that wouldn't be a bad idea."

"Oh, thanks!" said Joe. He told him how he and Mary Lou had been teaching Patch tricks and that the dog could already do two pretty well—shake hands and stand up on his hind legs. He added that he would take up the other dog's education right away, so that she, too, would be able to do something in the show. The time was short, he knew, as the bazaar was to be held in about three weeks. But he could try anyway.

"You'll have to have a really good show so people will crowd around and watch," Mr. West said. "Why don't you ask some other boys and girls with dogs to come in with you? Then you could have something worthwhile."

A wave of delight rolled over Joe. "I'll do that," he said. "We'll work up something swell—a real production. Gee, this will be fun!"

"The more people you get to applaud the dogs," the minister said, "the more chances you'll have of finding someone who wants your two."

"It's a truly super idea," Joe said. He thought about Mary Lou and wondered how it would strike her. But he felt fairly sure he could work things out to suit her, too. Then another idea struck him. A dog show would give him a fine chance to show his father how really wonderful dogs were. The whole trouble with his father was that he didn't take the time to get acquainted with dogs. Joe would ask him very specially to please come. There certainly were a lot of reasons for giving this dog show.

The truck had long vanished from sight. Other cars came and went and the road lay quiet and empty again.

Mr. West and Joe crossed, and as they were about to part, the minister said, "Come over to see me about this later on, Joe. We'll have to choose a place for the dog show at the bazaar grounds."

"Oh yes," said Joe. "I'll come and I'll bring some of the other kids with me so they can help us plan."

"Fine," said Mr. West. "Come Monday afternoon about four o'clock."

Joe felt wonderful now. Here was something solid to work on. He went directly to Dan's house, for Dan had the smart, eager little dog, Betsy, the Manchester and beagle crossbreed. She certainly must be in the show.

Joe found Dan in the far corner of his back yard under the big willow tree, making a work shed for himself out of old boxes and crates. Betsy came running to meet Joe, her tail wagging in hearty welcome. She flopped her front feet down, gave a little yap, then went tearing back to Dan. And again she rushed joyously at Joe.

Dan yelled out, "Hey, Joe! Look at what I'm making."

Joe came and looked. But interested as he ordinarily would have been, his thoughts could not concentrate on that just now and he burst out and told Dan all about the dog show instead. Dan stopped working and listened. It was the kind of idea he liked.

Joe said, "And your dog must be in the show, too, Dan."

"Sure," said Dan. "Of course, Betsy will have to be in it. She only does one trick, though. My family like the way she acts by herself. That's why we never taught her many tricks."

Joe said he thought one trick would be enough for her. Dan put away his hammer and he and Betsy and Joe set out to round up their friends and let them in on their undertaking. Betsy led the way, tail waving and ears flopping. She looked back at the boys every now and then to see where they wanted to go and then dashed ahead again. The boys went to Mary Lou's and, having collected her, hurried on to Phil's.

The four of them gathered under a tree on the

*Betsy came running to meet Joe, her tail wagging*

Applebys' lawn to talk things over all together.

"A show!" said Phil. Though he wasn't as fond of dogs as Joe and Dan, staging a performance of any kind —that was something he liked.

But Mary Lou looked serious. Joe asked her what was worrying her and, just as he had feared, she said that she thought that the whole plan was dangerous for her and Patch.

"What if someone besides my Mommie and Daddy sees Patch in the show and wants him?" she asked. "I'll lose him entirely, then."

"Well, it's this way," said Joe. "We'll only let Patch do his tricks when your mother and father are watching." Then, after a pause, he added, "But if they don't take Patch, Mary Lou, then I'll just have to let someone else have him. I can't keep him."

Mary Lou still resisted the idea of letting the dog be in the show but the boys kept assuring her that her parents probably would want Patch when they saw him perform, so she finally gave in.

Dan was interested in this problem between Mary Lou, her parents, Patch and the cat, Mike. He asked Mary Lou, "Your father isn't against Patch, too, is he? Wouldn't he take your side about Patch, if you asked him?"

"I have asked him," Mary Lou said, "lots of times. But he just says to do whatever Mommie decides about

58

it. And Mom is still mad about what Patch did to the living room the day he chased Mike."

Then Phil wanted to know how Mary Lou and Joe were getting along in the matter of training Patch to behave better toward cats.

Mary Lou explained, "The trouble isn't just that Patch chases Mike, it's Mike, too. Every time we get them together, he slaps Patch. And that gets Patch so excited he chases him."

Dan stretched out flat on his back on the grass. "They'd get used to each other if they were together in the same house every day. All you have to do is . . ."

Joe interrupted at this point. "Let's get back to planning our show," he said. "We have to get organized."

So they set to work. They decided among themselves which boys, girls and dogs were to be asked to take part. And they divided the business of inviting each of those agreed on.

Joe would ask the Applebys to let the boxer, Teddy, perform one of the tricks he knew. And, of course, he had Shaggy and Patch to train. Mary Lou had to work with him in training Patch and she was to ask the Wharton girls to enter their wire-haired terrier, Peppy, and to see that he practiced his tricks.

Phil would go after Nancy and her big Newfoundland, Jamie. And as Jamie's best stunt was done together with the dachshund named Honey, who lived next door to him, Phil undertook to ask for this dog, too.

Dan was to tell Jim about the show when he got back from the nearby big city where he had gone with his father. Jim was to bring his English setter, Pal. Dan had to telephone to Tom Jason up at the farm, too. Tom's hound, Rambler, wouldn't do any tricks. But Tom and his sisters would certainly want to come and see the show. Besides this, Dan had to prepare his own Betsy to do her one trick well in public.

Phil and Joe were elected show managers. They were going to be responsible for preparing the place where the show was to be given and for seeing that each dog did his stunt at the right time on the program.

When all this had been settled, Mary Lou said she had to go home. It was nearly six o'clock and would soon be dinner time, and she was hungry. The others were ready to leave, too, so the meeting broke up for the day.

Joe, arriving at his own home a few minutes later, found the house fragrant with his mother's cooking. He looked in at the study and found his father at his desk, working over some papers. Joe didn't disturb him. He just smiled contentedly, thinking about what he was going to show him at bazaar time and imagining how it was going to make Dad take more interest in dogs.

He went upstairs and washed and combed his hair,

60

and all the while he was filled with an inner glow.

When he came down Mother asked him to help carry dishes to the table and to call Father and Marty. So he did.

Later, when the family was eating dinner, he told them a little about the dog show and how it was to help him find homes for Shaggy and Patch.

Dr. and Mrs. Collins were delighted.

"Now you're getting somewhere," said Dr. Collins.

"We certainly are," said Joe, pleased.

For the next few weeks, Joe and his friends worked with their dogs every afternoon, perfecting their tricks. And right at the start a most surprising discovery was made.

Joe, Mary Lou, and Marty were in the Collins' back yard one day, working with Patch. Shaggy had been brought out to watch. She sat beside Joe, her ears perked up to sharp points, looking intensely interested. Suddenly, she went over to Patch and stood up on her hind legs in front of him without being asked.

"Look!" cried Joe. "Shaggy already knows this trick!"

"Gosh!" Mary Lou cried.

"Say, maybe she knows some more!" said Marty.

Joe picked up a stick to throw away. He was going to ask Shaggy to retrieve it. But Shaggy thought it was for another trick he knew. She jumped over the stick instead, as Joe held it in his hand.

"Hey!" he cried in amazement and held it a little higher. She jumped over it again.

"Good dog," said Joe, beaming.

Mary Lou and Marty sat down in the grass and petted the little dog and complimented her. She wagged practically all over.

"What a dog!" said Joe. "A trained trick-dog!"

They found next that she would lie down and roll over on command, too. And best of all, she looked so very happy when she did her tricks.

"Why, Shaggy will be the star of the show!" Marty exclaimed.

Joe and Mary Lou excitedly agreed. But the next moment Mary Lou was worrying about Patch again. She was afraid Shaggy would outshine him and so spoil Patch's chances with her mother.

But Joe had the solution to that problem. "Patch will do his tricks in the first half of the show and he'll be announced as the only dog to be given away in that time. That way he'll get all the attention. We'll give your father and mother a chance to take him right after he does his tricks, Mary Lou. Then we'll go on with the show and Shaggy will be the last performer in the second half. She'll be the climax."

So it was decided and everyone felt satisfied and very hopeful of the outcome.

The weeks went by quickly, not only for Joe and his

friends, but for the whole Collins family because they were all so busy. Mrs. Collins had shopping and sewing and packing to do, for the voyage to Europe with Dr. Collins. And she had to get the house in final order for Aunt Edna's coming. Besides that, she had to finish the bright print aprons she was making for the bazaar.

Marty and Joe helped her all they could with the everyday work about the house. And Marty did some of the sewing on the aprons, too, and helped Joe make a poster for the dog show. There was hardly an idle moment for anyone in the family until about the time that school was out.

All this while the two stray dogs were still in Joe's care, of course. But now that he had explained to his father about the show, and how he would give the dogs away then, Dr. Collins was not impatient about it.

"All right," he said when reminded of it. "I just hope it works."

## CHAPTER FIVE

# *Bazaar and Dog Show*

The Saturday of the bazaar Joe was up early. He went outdoors as soon as he was dressed and looked at the sky. It was fairly clear, just as the weather reports over the radio had said it would be. Soft gray tufts of clouds were drifting past but there was lots of blue sky beyond them. There was no threat of rain to spoil things. He whistled to himself cheerfully.

A little later that morning, when Joe, Marty and Mother had washed the breakfast dishes and made the beds, they got ready to go to the church to help prepare the bazaar. The dogs, Patch and Shaggy, were left at home. They would only be in the way if they came along so early in the day.

The Collinses had a number of things to load into the car. They took a card table and a white linen cover for it, and the stack of gay print aprons. Joe brought the poster Marty had made, and some other things for the show.

They drove by the Applebys' first and Phil came out carrying a large, loose bundle and a folded wooden frame.

"The things for the dog show," he said. The Collinses chatted with him as he put his things into the back of the car. Then he climbed in and they drove on.

At the church, they found a lot of women already busy on the broad green grounds between this building and the minister's house. Some were setting up tables, some were tying bright strips of red and white bunting from tree to tree. Boxes and baskets of cakes and cookies were being brought from cars and set down to be unpacked later. Children's dresses, pot-holders, painted mats and other odds and ends were being spread on the other tables, ready for sale.

Joe carried his mother's card table to the lawn. Mrs. Collins and Marty brought the aprons and other things. Then Joe and Phil took their bundle and carried it to the far end of the bazaar grounds where Mr. West, the minister, had given them all the space they needed for their dog show.

Phil's bundle was a red and white beach cabaña which he had borrowed from some neighbors who had a summer place on the New Jersey shore. He and Joe set it up together, then they pegged out white sticks in a circle, beginning at the two sides of the cabaña and reaching out from there.

Red and white tapes were strung around these, making a ring about ten feet across. One by one the dogs were to be brought into the cabaña, which was propped up with two sticks in the back. They were to appear from there to do their stunts in the ring.

"It'll look fine that way," Phil said. "Like a theater, with a curtain and all." And he added, "The front flap's the curtain."

"Yes, it's swell," Joe agreed.

Next the boys put up their poster. They tacked it on a tree right in the midst of the tables in the busiest part

66

of the bazaar grounds, so that everyone would see it. The notice read:

## D O G   S H O W

*At three o'clock this afternoon*
The Two Dogs with Ribbons on Their Collars
Will Be Given Away Free
*Absolutely   Free!*

Dan, Mary Lou, Nancy and Jim came to the grounds, too, after a while and stood around and talked and planned with Joe and Phil.

At noon everyone straggled off home to lunch.

The Collinses had a cold lunch of sandwiches and salad and milk which Mother had prepared that morning.

They ate it somewhat hurriedly, all except Dr. Collins, who, it seemed to Joe, had no idea how important and interesting this day was.

Afterward, when Dr. Collins started to leave, to get back to his laboratory again, Joe hurried to him and said, "Dad, you're coming to our dog show this afternoon, aren't you?"

"You don't need me for that, do you?" Dr. Collins asked.

"Of course, we do," Joe said.

"I'll try, Joe," Dr. Collins assured him. "But if I don't get there, you'll just have to count me out. These are busy days for me."

"Please come," said Joe earnestly.

"I'll try," Dr. Collins promised. "What time does it start?"

"Three o'clock," Joe said.

"All right," Dr. Collins said as he picked up his brief case and went out the front door.

Mother and Marty went off, too, a half hour later. They had to get back to the bazaar to help put the finishing touches to the tables and greet the first-comers. Joe stayed behind with the dogs to wait till nearly show-time.

About two o'clock Mary Lou came over. She brushed Patch to make his tan coat shine a little more. Patch was surprised at the vigor with which she brushed, and didn't like it very much. He preferred to jump around. Mary Lou had quite a time getting him slicked up, and tying the blue satin ribbon on his collar.

Joe, who was meanwhile working on the much more cooperative Shaggy, had to laugh at the way Patch acted.

"He's a clown," he said.

"I know and I like him that way," said Mary Lou.

The other stray dog loved being brushed. She seemed to know something interesting was going to happen that day. She turned this way and that, as Joe asked her to, and looked at him eagerly and questioningly. The hair stuck out gayly and fuzzily around her little face.

Joe had some trouble with the pink ribbon for Shaggy's collar, though. He couldn't make a nice bow, so Mary Lou tied it for him. Then, shortly before three o'clock, they put the leashes on the two dogs and set out for the bazaar.

On the way, they met a cat coming down the sidewalk and Patch reared up and fanned the air with his front feet.

"Gosh!" said Joe.

"Patch! Stop!" Mary Lou cried.

They were a little worried that Patch still got so excited about cats, when they had been trying to get him over that for weeks.

"At least he doesn't bark at them anymore," Mary Lou said.

"That's right," Joe agreed. "And that's something."

When they arrived at the church, quite a large crowd of men, women and children had already gathered. Everything looked festive, the tables with their variety of wares, the red and white bunting that was strung from the trees, the bright summer clothes of the women and girls. There was a hum of talk in the air, as people roamed around, looking at the things that were spread on the tables and buying whatever they liked.

## The Right Dog for Joe

The cakes, cookies and pies, which Joe had noticed with such interest that morning, were now on the tables. He felt in his pocket for his money, thinking he would like to buy some to eat right away. But then he decided he had better attend to the dog show first. Anyway, his mother had said she was going to buy one of Mrs. Carney's coconut layer cakes and bring it home for supper. So he put the laden tables out of mind. He and Mary Lou skirted the crowd with their dogs and took them into the show ring.

A nice chorus of barking was under way there, for Dan was already at hand with his Betsy, and Nancy with her Newfoundland, Jamie and the two Wharton girls with Peppy, the wire-haired terrier. Phil was holding the dachshund, Honey. Jim stood nearby with his setter. He had brought him to see the show, though he had decided not to enter him. "He's stage-shy," he had told Joe.

A number of people were already crowding around to see what was going on here. And among them was Tom Jason with his sisters, Ellen and Charlotte.

"Gee," said Tom, a rangy redhead. "I sure do wish our Rambler could have been in this show."

"He'd be scared of this crowd," said Charlotte, who was about Marty's age. "We couldn't even bring him down to watch."

"He only likes us and you, Joe," little Ellen added. "He doesn't like to be with a lot of strangers. He's used

70

to our farm."

"He's okay," Joe said. "Not all dogs have to do tricks. Rambler is okay the way he is."

Joe, Phil and Dan hurriedly made last minute preparations. Mary Lou went in search of her mother. And Joe kept an eye out for her return. He felt a pleasurable relief when he saw her coming back through the crowd, with both Mr. and Mrs. Denis in tow. Mrs. Denis, he noticed, did not look too enthusiastic but at least she had come. As for Mr. Denis, his face was positively sour. It did not look too hopeful. Still, Patch could try to win them.

Joe signaled to Phil, and Phil raised his hand to the other boys and girls who stood behind the cabaña trying to keep their dogs quiet. His signal meant that they should hold themselves in readiness, as the show was about to start.

Joe, the announcer, stood in the ring. Phil went into the cabaña, to help each dog in under the propped-up back when his turn came and then send him on into the ring. Dan stood in front, ready to draw up the entrance flap which served as a curtain.

"The first thing on the program," Joe announced over the barking of the boxer and the setter, "is a stunt by the Newfoundland, Jamie, and the dachshund, Honey."

Nancy came out of the cabaña with them, serious in her important duty.

She ordered, "Down, Jamie." The Newfoundland, a

great, patient hulk of a dog, lay down and put his nose on his paws. She said to the dachshund, "Up on Jamie, Honey," and the small, earnest dog clambered to the big dog's back. The Newfoundland rose to his feet then, his eyes and his jowls so droopy and solemn-looking you could hardly tell how pleased he was. And then Nancy led him slowly around the ring with Honey riding on his back.

Everyone clapped as they came to a stop. Nancy took the dachshund off the Newfoundland's back, the dogs went into the cabaña with her and Dan let the curtain drop behind them.

In this first pause in the show, Joe looked to see if his own family was in the audience. A big crowd had gathered around the ring now, and yes, there they were, fairly close to the front. And his father really had come. He stood between Marty and Mother, his face serious. Joe gave his family a quick smile and went on about his business.

Patch was next on the program, and as Mr. and Mrs. Denis were watching, this was a very important part of the show. Phil let Patch out and Joe greeted and petted him to start him off right.

He took Patch into the center of the ring, touched his front legs and said, "Sit up, Patch!"

But Patch didn't sit up. He turned his laughing face up to Joe, lolling his tongue, and then began to bark and

72

leap around him playfully.

"Hey, stop that, Patch!" Joe cried worriedly.

Patch quieted down for a moment and then Joe tried him with his trick again. But Patch acted as though he had never even heard of the trick. Joe tried the second stunt, hoping he remembered that better.

"Shake hands," he said, taking hold of one of Patch's front paws. But the dog just rolled over on his back in the grass and waved his legs in the air.

Laughter bubbled through the crowd. And Joe heard his father's voice. "What a dog to try to train," he said, chuckling. "An individualist. A non-cooperator."

Mary Lou dashed into the ring to see if she could make Patch behave. But no, he wouldn't do his tricks at all in front of the audience.

Joe was in despair. Their whole plan for Patch had failed. Not only would Mrs. Denis remain uninterested now, but probably no one else would take Patch either. He looked at Mary Lou and saw that she was crying.

73

She had drawn Patch to one side of the ring and sat there holding him, with her cheek against his head. The audience had stopped laughing and there was silence, broken only by murmurs of sympathy.

It was a very sad moment.

Then Joe heard Mary Lou's father call out, "Mary Lou, don't cry. It doesn't matter about Patch not doing his tricks. You can surely have him if you want him that badly! Can't she, Lucy?" And he turned to Mrs. Denis.

Mrs. Denis burst into a warm laugh. "All right," she said, "I give up. You can have your dog, Mary Lou, honey. For goodness' sake, stop crying."

What a surprise! Joe could hardly believe his ears. Patch had won them over in spite of himself!

Mary Lou's face broke into a damp but very happy smile. She gathered up Patch, who was quite an armful for her, and set him over the tapes and led him to her father and mother. There she and the dog took their places, looking entirely satisfied.

Joe stood in the center of the ring then and announced, "The first of the dogs that were to be given away, has been accepted by the Denises."

Everybody clapped. And the show went on.

Peppy, the wire-haired terrier, and Teddy, the boxer, were brought out. Barbara held up a stick almost a foot from the ground and Peppy jumped over it, ran around back of her and jumped over it again. He was so enthusiastic about doing this that he hardly stopped a moment. And when Barbara laid the stick down, he looked very much disappointed.

Then Joe tossed a light rubber ball to Teddy, the boxer. He caught it expertly in his mouth. Joe had to wrestle with him to get the ball away so that he could toss it to him once more. The tussle for the ball was half the fun to the boxer.

After another minute or two of this stunt, both Peppy and Teddy retired.

Dan and his Betsy were next on the program. Dan brought out a low wooden footstool and set it down in the ring. He spread a white linen napkin on it. Now it was a dog's dining table. He called Betsy and she trotted over to him. Her black coat shone like satin, her face was full of eagerness to play with Dan. He led her to the little table and said, "Sit down, Betsy."

She sat down before the table and looked at Dan, then opened her mouth in a wide yawn, showing her pink gums and tongue and making a small sound that was like an attempt to talk to him.

"She says the service is slow," suggested a man in the audience, and a lilt of laughter went up.

Dan grinned and put a small dog biscuit on the table before Betsy and said firmly, "Don't touch it yet." She sat there looking at it, her mouth watering, but waiting patiently. Finally, Dan said, "Take it!" and Betsy took

75

it up daintily with her mouth, ate it and then examined the tablecloth to see if she had dropped a single crumb. She looked very earnest and a bit proud, as though she always ate at tables. Everybody clapped and chuckled.

"It's just a little trick," Dan said.

"But she does it mighty nice," said a woman.

Dan led Betsy away, pleased because the people liked her so.

Mac, a Scotty, came next, led by a boy named Johnny. This boy and dog had been asked to enter the show only the day before, when Joe had accidentally discovered Mac's talents. Johnny asked Mac to "talk" for the audience and he barked softly in response. He asked Mac to "sing." The dog threw back his head and gave a high quavering wail—a lovely tenor he had, and was much appreciated by all.

Then came the final act of the show, which was Shaggy's. Joe hoped with all his might that she wouldn't do as Patch had and forget her tricks before the crowd. He led her out somewhat fearfully.

But Shaggy didn't forget anything. Joe told her to get up on her hind legs and she did it. And then she walked halfway across the ring in that position, holding her front paws up very gracefully, and lolling her pink tongue out at one side. Joe let her rest a moment, then signaled to Dan, who pulled a harmonica out of his pocket and began to play a tune.

76

*Dan began to play a tune. Joe said, "Dance, Shaggy!"*

Joe said, "Dance, Shaggy!" She got up on her hind legs again and stepped sidewise, this way and that, and turned around several times. Everyone laughed, and a man asked, "Is that one of the dogs you are giving away?"

"It is," answered Joe. "Want her?"

"Yes, sir!" said the man. "That's a smart dog. I want her for my little girl, Sue, here," and he pointed to the three-year-old child beside him. "And for myself and my wife, too," he added. "I'll take her all right. She's a wonderful little dog."

"Okay, she's yours," Joe said quickly, before the man could change his mind.

"We will just love having her," said his wife.

Another woman in the crowd said, "I'm sorry I didn't speak up first. I'd like to have had her, too."

"So would I," said a tall young man.

Joe told them he was very sorry he didn't have more dogs to give away just now.

Then he announced, "The show isn't quite over. Shaggy can do more tricks." And he put the little stubby dog through a few more. She rolled over on her back at his command, then jumped through a hoop several times and finally shook hands with Joe.

Once more the crowd clapped. Then some of them started to move away.

Shaggy's new owners, the Averys, stayed behind playing with the dog and getting acquainted with her.

78

The boys and girls who had dogs in the show took them home now, for the dogs were getting more and more excited and the barking was loud and long.

Joe stood in the ring, feeling very pleased that the show had gone off so well—and especially that it had served its purpose for Shaggy and Patch. They both had permanent homes now at last.

Mary Lou and Patch were still standing around. And now she came over to Joe and said, "Thanks for helping me get Patch, Joe."

"That's okay," Joe answered with a grin. "He's kind of been yours all along, anyway."

"Yes, he has," said Mary Lou, and ran away with Patch. "Good-bye!"

Joe looked about for his family. His mother and sister were still there, watching and talking to friends. But his father had left. Joe felt disappointed. He was afraid Dad still wasn't as much interested in dogs as Joe wanted him to be. He had just gone off without saying a word.

Well, anyway, the show had been a real success and Joe was happy about that.

The Averys were getting ready to leave, too, and Mr. Avery asked Joe, "Would you come home with us and carry Shaggy, so she won't be scared? We live just a little way from here."

"Yes," said Joe. "I'd like to come."

The little girl offered, "I'll carry the doggie."

But her mother said, "Not yet, Sue. Let Joe hold her till she gets used to you."

Joe attached Shaggy's leash, and they went to the Averys' car which was parked a block from the church.

As they drove away, Joe said, "After supper I'll bring you the old rug Shaggy's been sleeping on. It'll make her feel more at home."

Mr. and Mrs. Avery thought this was a very good idea.

"Shaggy had a dirty old felt hat she always kept with her when I first found her," Joe went on to say, "but she doesn't need it anymore."

"That's good," said Mr. Avery. "We'd just as soon do without the hat if it's dirty." And he chuckled.

Mrs. Avery opened a bag of cookies she had bought at the bazaar and gave one to Joe and one to her little girl.

"Sue, you can give just a little piece to the dog to make friends," she said.

Sue fed bits of cookie to Shaggy, who sat in Joe's lap. Shaggy liked both the cookie and the little girl. Soon she put her front feet in Sue's lap and stood there, half on her and half on Joe.

Everything was going to be all right for Shaggy, Joe could see, just as it was for Patch. And both dogs were going to live fairly near Joe's house. He could see them whenever he wanted to.

CHAPTER SIX

# *A Morning with a Bad Twist on It*

AT BREAKFAST the next morning the talk was all of Dr. and Mrs. Collins' voyage to France. It was already the first week of July, and the liner on which they had

81

reservations was sailing in five days.

Marty and Joe had many questions to ask their parents, questions about things they wanted to do that summer, about household arrangements that were to be made when Aunt Edna came to take charge.

It was a fine hot day, and breakfast was particularly pleasant because school was out and no one had to hurry off. Everyone looked comfortable and cheerful except Joe. His mouth turned downward just a little at the corners.

Marty looked at him, as she buttered a fresh piece of toast, and asked, "What's the matter with you, Joe? You're awfully quiet for you."

"Aw, nothing," said Joe. "It's just that the house feels funny without any dogs at all."

"Oh, nonsense," said Dr. Collins.

Mrs. Collins laughed. "It won't hurt you to be without a dog for a few months, Joe," she said. "And, anyway, you'll be going to Sky Inn in less than two weeks, so you won't really have much time to worry about it."

At that Joe's face lighted. "Oh, yes!" he exclaimed, "Sky Inn! That's something!"

"By the way," said Dr. Collins, "I want to compliment you on that dog show you and your friends staged. It was great—and a good way to find masters for your strays."

"Thanks," said Joe.

Marty and Mother complimented him, too. Marty said, "Dogs are really very nice, Dad. You're missing something, not being interested in them as much as the rest of us."

"Maybe," said Dr. Collins. "But I like them well enough."

Joe said nothing, but he didn't think his father liked dogs enough at all.

The family had finished breakfast and now they left the table.

Joe had plans of his own. He kicked down the wrinkled cuff of one leg of his khaki pants and started to the front door, calling back to his mother, "Guess I'll go out and see what's doing." He had to get together with Phil and talk about Sky Inn. But before that he would just check up on how Shaggy and Patch were getting along in their new homes.

First he visited the Averys, and found Shaggy very cheerful. She wagged her tail vigorously for Joe, and licked his hands. But she liked her new family, too, Joe could see, and would soon be completely at home there.

He went to the Denises' next. As Patch was already devoted to Mary Lou, no real trouble was to be expected there, except perhaps with the cat. He would just ask her about that.

Coming to Mary Lou's house, he found her at home, and she showed him how things were. The cat, Mike, calmly dozing, sat on the mantle in the living room, well out of the dog's reach. Patch was paying no attention to him at all.

"He's getting used to him," Mary Lou said happily, "and Mike will get friendly soon, I think. This morning he ate a little out of Patch's dish while Patch was still eating."

That was real progress, all right. Joe felt he wasn't needed especially at the Denises' anymore, so he headed for the Carneys' next. Mrs. Carney had come down from the Inn in the mountains to take Phil back with her, now that school was out. And, in about a week, Joe himself would be going up there. He could hardly wait for that time to come!

He arrived in high spirits at the Carneys' old-fashioned white frame house, with the quaint-looking trim around the top of the front porch. At the door he called, "Phil! Hi, Phil!"

Phil answered from upstairs in a jubilant voice and came running down.

"I've got news!" he shouted. "Boy, have I got news!"

"What news?" Joe asked, catching the excitement.

In a burst of enthusiasm, Phil told him that his mother had just received a letter from Grandpa Carney, who owned a ranch in Arizona. Grandpa had asked her to let Phil come out there for the summer and his mother had agreed to let him go. The whole summer's plans

84

were changed, and he was leaving just as fast as he could.

"A ranch!" cried Joe. That was swell for Phil.

"Ma says I've been around the Inn too much," Phil explained. "She wants me to see something different for a change. And this way I sure will see something different, living on a ranch all summer! Oh boy!"

Mrs. Carney was coming down the stairs. "Isn't that great news?" she said to Joe. "Phil will have a real chance to see the West. And he'll ride horses and work with cowhands."

"Gee!" Joe said. But his spirits were beginning to sink very low. "Then I guess I can't go up to visit Phil at Sky Inn this summer."

There was a sudden silence.

"Well, I guess not," said Phil lamely. "I was so glad I was going to the ranch, I almost forgot that. Gee, I'm sorry, Joe. But you can come up next summer. I'll be there next summer."

Mrs. Carney added, "I've been thinking about that. And I'm awfully sorry, Joe. But you wouldn't want Phil to miss going West, would you?"

"Of course not," said Joe.

"And we'll really make it up to you next year, for letting you down this time," Mrs. Carney promised.

"Thanks," said Joe. "Don't worry about me." But he felt very sad. Going to the Inn in the mountains had been the one exciting thing planned for his vacation.

85

And now he had just nothing at all to look forward to. He hoped he did not show his disappointment too much, and decided to leave before Mrs. Carney and Phil should notice how badly he felt. So, after a few more minutes of talk, he said he had to go home. He left, walking purposely erect, but the farther he got from the Carneys' house, the more his head drooped and his feet dragged. Gloom descended on him fully.

What a thing to have happen! What a deal!

Joe, arriving at home, found his mother in the kitchen. He told her about the Carneys' change of summer plans with a lump in his throat. Mother was as sorry about it as Joe was. But she did advise him to go on and find something to do and not to sit around the house and feel sorry for himself.

"Because there's just nothing we can do about it," she said.

"I know," Joe agreed. But knowing it didn't make him feel any better.

"Set the ironing board up for me, will you, dear? I have some dresses to press."

All the next day Joe went on feeling downhearted. Preparations for Mother's and Father's departure were going on, and the whole town was beginning to be stripped of friends. So many of them were going away with their families, this warm month of July, for vacations in other places. There would be nothing at all for

86

him but staying at home.

Marty did not seem to mind. Her best boy and girl friends were going to be in Brewster Hills all summer, so she really wanted to stay, too.

Phil was to leave for Arizona on Thursday, and Joe went down to his house to say good-bye.

It was painful to Joe, to watch Phil getting off for his exciting vacation. But, still, he just couldn't stay away from the Carneys this morning.

When he came into the house, Mrs. Carney greeted him in her usual friendly way. She was going to go back up to Sky Inn the day after tomorrow herself, she told him, and would not be back the rest of the season.

Joe waited around and watched Phil close his suitcase and small trunk, and then helped him put them into the car. He felt sorrier for himself moment by moment. Then Mrs. Carney came out, handed Phil the jacket of his suit, and they got into the car.

"Want to drive to the station with us, Joe?" Mrs. Carney invited.

Joe shook his head. As the car started, he called out "Good-bye" once more, and Phil held up his hand in farewell. In a minute the Carneys' car disappeared around the corner of the tree-lined street, and Joe started dolefully home.

Teddy, the Applebys' boxer, lying under a shady tree, saw Joe and came trotting out to walk with him a little way. Joe was very glad of his company. Two blocks farther on, as the pair passed the Healys', Joe noticed Mr. Henry Healy out on the grounds. He was clipping withered flowers from a bush. Joe was too much concerned with his own troubles to pay much attention to him.

But then Teddy saw a squirrel on the lawn and dashed after it, passing close to Mr. Healy. As it happened, Mr. Healy just had a branch in his hand, which he had broken from the bush. He angrily struck the dog with it, saying, "Get out of here!" And with a yelp, Teddy ran off toward his own home.

Joe, already unhappy because his summer's plans were broken up, felt a sharp new anger rise in him. "Some day I'm going to pay Mr. Healy back for the way he treats dogs," he said to himself, as he went on. But he could not think of anything he could do. He was just terribly angry.

At home, Joe set to work and raked the cut grass from the lawn, as his father had asked him to, and took it away in the wheelbarrow. He tried not to think about Mr. Healy, but the man kept coming into his mind.

After supper that night, Joe was on his way to Jim's house with his trumpet. He and Jim were going to practice and try to make the school band next year. As Joe neared Mr. Healy's house again, he suddenly had a notion as to what he wanted to do to him. The casement

*He felt sorrier for himself moment by moment*

windows of the dining room were dark. Lights showed only in the living room and upstairs. The Healys were probably upstairs, Joe thought, for the living room was clearly empty.

He slipped around into the street, which lay on the side of the house where the dining room was. Hiding behind the hedge, he picked up a stone and threw it at the dark windows. It struck one of the small panes, and there was a clatter and tinkle of glass.

Joe heard Mrs. Healy call to her husband in a startled voice, "Henry, someone just broke one of the windows downstairs! Threw a rock, I think."

Then Joe, running off down the side street in the darkness, heard Mr. Healy, with his head out of a second-floor window, shout angrily, "Who's there? Who did that?"

It was too dark for him to see Joe, and in another minute the boy was quite a distance away, for he was a good, fast runner. He made his way around the next block to get back to the street that led to Jim's house. No one had seen Joe. No one at all knew that he had broken the window.

Momentarily, he felt glad he had done it. His anger at Mr. Healy seemed partly wiped out with this act. But long before he arrived at Jim's house, his pleasure gave way to a feeling of complete discontent. Breaking windows was a childish thing to do, he knew. It gave

90

him no lasting satisfaction at all. And what was more, it would not improve Mr. Healy's attitude toward dogs in any way.

At Jim's house, a little later, Joe and his friend practiced on their trumpets for a while. But Joe's heart was not in the work tonight, and he went home before long.

The next day, Mrs. Collins asked Joe and Marty to help in the house again. While he worked, Joe was far from cheerful, for he kept thinking about Sky Inn and all the fun he would miss because he could not go up there this summer. And when he thought of his window-breaking at the Healys', he felt still worse.

One of the things he and Marty had to do was to get Aunt Edna's room ready for her. But they did not start at this, for one reason or another, until the latter part of the afternoon. Aunt Edna preferred to sleep on the ground floor, the Collinses knew from past visits, so they were preparing the spare bedroom in back of the study for her. Joe and Marty were shoving the bed out from the wall when they heard Mrs. Carney's voice at the front door.

"Anybody home?" she called.

Mrs. Collins and Joe hurried to the front door and Marty trailed on behind.

Mrs. Carney came in with sighs and gasps. "The way I've worked today! I'm all in. It's a good thing that I have dependable help up at the Inn or I couldn't stay away from there such a large part of the week."

"You do have your hands full," Mrs. Collins sympathized.

And Mrs. Carney, sinking onto the couch, grateful for a moment's rest, said, "Thank goodness I've got Phil off to Arizona. This summer out there is going to be awfully good for him. And that brings me around to what I came here for."

"Yes?" Mrs. Collins said inquiringly.

"I've been thinking," Mrs. Carney said. "You know I'm going to miss not having Phil around at Sky Inn to do odd jobs for me and run errands. I was wondering whether Joe might like to come up for the whole summer and sort of take Phil's place?"

Joe almost burst with joy. He said, "Of course, I'd like to. For the whole summer! Oh, boy!"

Mrs. Collins laughed. "There's your answer," she said. "And I certainly would be most happy to have him there with you."

"Fine," said Mrs. Carney. "Then it's settled. I'll pay him a little for the odd jobs he'll do for me, of course."

"Oh, I'd just like to come. You don't have to pay me," Joe said. "I just like to be up there."

"Well, I wouldn't let you work for me for nothing, Joe," Mrs. Carney said. "You won't get rich on the jobs I have for you. But you'll have a little money saved up at the end of the summer." She turned to Mrs. Collins. "I'm surely glad he's coming. I like a boy around the place."

Then she asked if Joe could get ready in time to drive up to the Inn with her the next day. And Marty volunteered to help him pack because her mother was so busy getting herself and Dr. Collins off to Europe.

Dr. Collins came in then and was told the news.

"Well, that's great," he declared. A smile flickered briefly over his face. "A mountaintop many miles from any town. That's a fine place for Joe this summer, for at least there won't be any stray dogs for him to collect."

"Oh, you can be sure of that," Mrs. Carney said, laughing. "There'll be no such problems at Sky Inn."

Marty, who had done more listening than talking so far, put in, "Now everybody's leaving Brewster Hills but me." But she sounded so perfectly content that Joe could see that she had good plans of her own, right here. He was glad he didn't have to be sorry for her, staying behind, glad there was nothing to mar his happiness at his own good luck.

He was going up into the mountains to Sky Inn, and he wasn't just going for two weeks, but for the whole summer! He was sorry he had wasted so much time being sad for the last few days. Everything was just fine.

## CHAPTER SEVEN

# *Up in the Mountains*

SKY INN stood at the very top of Lookout Mountain, with other wooded mountains and valleys rising and falling on every side as far as the eye could see. There was not a sign of other people living anywhere, except in the valley toward the east, seven miles or so away. Here, several farms lay, their white houses and big red barns and silos

94

looking small, because of the distance.

Beyond the farms, another mountain rose; and if one could have looked into the valley just east of it, one would have found there the very small town of a few hundred people, called Truley. It had a post office and a few stores, but was connected with the distant railroad only by bus, truck and car. People who came to Sky Inn for their vacations usually drove up in their own cars. But some came to Truley by bus and were met by Dick, the handyman, in the Carneys' car or station wagon.

It was the high aloneness of the Inn that made it such a wonderful and exciting place to Joe, and so it was to most of the other visitors, too. Many of the guests came back to Sky Inn year after year.

When Joe arrived with Mrs. Carney, he quickly made himself useful around the place. Every morning he swept the long porch that reached around three sides of the great stone house, and cleaned the path that led to the road. He mowed the lawn and weeded the vegetable garden and flower borders on certain days. Sometimes there were errands to do in the town; then he drove to Truley with Dick, and the two of them attended to matters there. Joe tried hard to do everything Phil would have done, had he been at the Inn to help his mother.

There were often other special ways in which Mrs. Carney called on Joe for help, too. Yet there were always lots of free hours for him every day. Then he played with whatever children were at the Inn at the time, and now and then he went on picnics or tramps with some of the guests, or he went fishing. Guests usually stayed about two weeks; and when they left, new ones came. Often Joe hated to see these vacation friends leave. But again there was always the interest of new people arriving, new ones to get acquainted with.

Just now, among the latest comers, he liked best the two children, Linda and Bert Harvey, and their parents. Another of his favorites was Dr. Graham, the thin, gray-haired man who kept much to himself, reading or just looking out over the mountains.

Letters from Phil began to arrive after the first week. Most of them were addressed to his mother, but a few to Joe, too. Mrs. Carney and Joe always read the letters together. Phil was having a wonderful time on the ranch, that was certain. But Joe did not envy him now. He did not want to be anywhere but up here in the mountains.

Every week there were air-mail letters from his father and mother in France, also; and sometimes, but less often, he heard from Marty and Cousin Edna. Everybody seemed to be having a good summer.

One August morning Joe was going up to the big house, after finishing a job of weeding in the tomato rows beyond the back lawn. All was quiet in the late morning sunlight. Insects buzzed about; a grasshopper popped up from the grass close to Joe's feet. The cows were grazing

96

peacefully in the west pasture, and as Joe looked in that
direction, he saw a big tan dog crossing the meadow at
the far end, making for the road.

"A collie," Joe said to himself. "I wonder whose dog
he is?"

He went on toward the house, then looked back once
more. There was the dog standing still, his ears alert,
looking at him. Joe wondered where he had come from.
It was a long way from the nearest farm, and the little
town in the second valley to the east was seven miles
away. A dog wasn't likely to wander up here all the way

97

from Truley. Maybe he belonged to some summer people picnicking near by.

As Joe stepped up on the back porch, Mrs. Carney came to the kitchen door, and said: "Well, Joe, you've done a long morning's work. Come and have a glass of milk and a sandwich. When a boy does weeding, he works up an appetite. At least that's what Phil always told me."

"I'm hungry all right." Joe grinned. He looked at his hands. They were stained black and green from holding the hoe handle and from pulling weeds.

He went to the faucet on the back lawn and washed, splashing the cold water over his face, too. It felt good. There was a roll of paper towels on the back porch and he dried himself.

"I'm certainly earning a lot of money, Mrs. Carney," Joe said. "I've got almost fifteen dollars now."

"That's a nice lot of money all right," said Mrs. Carney. "It'll come in handy sometime."

He and Mrs. Carney went into the kitchen. There, large, blonde Mrs. Mullens was already at work preparing lunch.

Mrs. Carney had set a glass of milk out on the table for Joe, and now she cut slices of bread and put butter and plum jam on them. Joe watched, getting hungrier every minute.

"I kind of miss Phil," Mrs. Carney said. "I always like

to see Phil eat. He enjoys it so. It's a good thing you're here to fill in for him."

The large jam sandwich was ready and Mrs. Carney handed it to Joe.

"Thanks," he said, and bit into it, and then drank some of the cold milk.

Mrs. Mullens, who was the cook, said, "Joe, those children, Linda and Bert, were looking for you a minute ago."

"Where'd they go?" Joe asked. He was eager to play with them, now that he was through with his work. Linda was only nine, and Bert was two years younger, but still they were fun.

"The children went out the front way," Mrs. Carney put in, "and across the road."

"Maybe they're at the brook," Mrs. Mullens said.

Joe finished his sandwich slowly. It tasted so good, he did not want the eating to be over too soon. As he sat there, his thoughts roved from one thing to another. He remembered the big dog he had just seen in the pasture. He thought about Dick, the young man who worked around the place this summer, who had driven to the railroad station at the little town earlier that morning. He would be back soon with some summer guests. Joe thought about his father and mother in Europe, and about his sister Marty, and wondered what all of them were doing right now. He had had a letter from Marty a few days ago. She seemed to be getting along all right at home in Brewster Hills.

He ate every crumb of the jam sandwich. He tipped his head back and turned the glass upside down to get the last drop of milk. Then he set it down and said, "That was good!" and went out to the front porch.

Some of the summer people were sitting there. One lady was knitting, another was looking at a magazine. Dr. Graham sat a little apart, as usual, looking out over the mountains.

Across the road were the Harvey children, Linda and Bert, and young Mr. and Mrs. Murray, whom Joe liked especially, and several other people. And at the far end of the patch of grass and weeds was the collie Joe had seen in the cow pasture a little while ago. He was looking the people over, shy, reserved, and keeping his distance. The children and grown-ups were trying to make friends with the dog, but he stood aside from them.

Linda saw Joe and called, "Come and see this big beautiful dog."

Joe went out to the field. What a fine-looking collie he was, the proud way he held his head, his eyes serious and yet eager. He looked young; probably he was not more than a year old.

One of the summer people said, "He isn't very friendly. Shy, I guess."

"He won't let anyone touch him at all," said little Bert.

Mr. and Mrs. Murray went toward the dog, coaxing him to come to them. He moved away and made for the brush.

Joe said in a low friendly tone, "Don't be scared of us, fellow."

The dog stopped and looked at him a moment, then quickly turned and trotted across to him. He trotted between the people, but paid no attention to any of them. He headed straight for Joe.

Joe put his hands out and stroked the collie's head. "Hello," he said. And the young collie wagged his tail and stayed close beside him.

"That's surprising," said slender, blonde Mrs. Murray. "Why, the dog acts as though he knew you, Joe."

"I guess he knows I like him, specially," Joe said.

"He isn't afraid of you at all," Linda remarked wonderingly.

Bert ran around in excitement. "He's Joe's dog!" he cried. "He's Joe's dog!"

Joe smiled happily, and kept stroking the collie and looking him over with increasing interest. The dog's head was not over-narrow; it was a fine and noble head, and looked very intelligent, too. His golden-brown and white coat was creamy in tone, and silky to the touch.

"I wish he did belong to me," Joe said. "I sure wish he did."

He led the dog to the porch and called to Mrs. Carney,

"Please come here a minute and see this collie."

Mrs. Carney answered from far back in the house, and shortly she came to the door.

"Why, where did that dog come from?" she asked, looking surprised.

All the summer guests began to talk. One man suggested that the collie must belong to some farmer in the region. But Mrs. Carney said she knew the dogs for miles around there, and this one did not belong to any of the farmers she was pretty sure.

"Besides," she said, "he looks more like a town dog than a farm dog. His coat is so sleek and his manners are so gentle." She didn't know just where he could have come from, she admitted, but surely not all the way from the little town of Truley.

Mrs. Murray's deep blue eyes were full of sympathy for the dog. She said, "I think some thoughtless person just dropped him from a car in passing by. He looks lost to me. Somebody probably got tired of taking care of him and set him out here on the mountaintop to get rid of him."

"Oh, no," said Joe. "Nobody could do a thing like that to a fine dog like this."

"He's got no collar on," tall, heavy-set Mr. Murray pointed out. "No license tag. The people who owned him probably took them off so the dog could not be traced back to them."

102

*Joe talked to the dog and he came along quietly*

## The Right Dog for Joe

"How could anybody be so mean," Linda cried.

The wiry, gray-haired doctor came over. "There are plenty of thoughtless people who would do just that," he said.

"My goodness," said Mrs. Carney, "do you folks really think he's a lost dog? And me assuring Dr. Collins Joe wouldn't find any strays away up here!"

Joe asked, "If this dog stays here, Mrs. Carney, and if no one comes for him in the next few days, don't you want him for yourself? He wouldn't be any trouble."

"Well, no," said Mrs. Carney. "We don't really want a dog, Joe. But he looks lost, and he's probably hungry. Bring him around to the back and we'll see if he wants something to eat."

Joe was eager to feed the dog, and he, with Linda and Bert following, started around to the back door. Joe talked to the dog, and he came along quietly, staying very close beside him.

Mrs. Carney went through the house to the kitchen. In a minute she came out with a dish of leftover cold meat and vegetables and set it down on the floor of the back porch. "There," she said.

The dog went up to the dish. He did not eat, but his mouth was watering and he trembled slightly with eagerness.

Joe patted him. "It's for you," he said. "Eat it, fellow."

The collie wagged his tail and began to eat quickly. It

104

was clear that he was very hungry.

"Well, did you ever?" cried Mrs. Carney. "So hungry! And he was too polite to eat without being told to. Did you ever!"

"That's just like Dan's dog, Betsy," Joe said. "I love a dog that's polite."

Bert and Linda sat down in the grass and watched. The collie went on eating. He ate fast but daintily. When the dish was empty, he lifted his head a moment. Then he licked the plate all over again, though there was not a bit left.

"He was hungry all right," Joe said, and then added, "I hope no one claims him, so we can keep him here at least a little while."

The young collie stayed around the Inn and played with Joe and Linda and Bert all the rest of the day. He played in the barn with them and he trotted along with them when they went fishing in the brook. Joe gave him a name—he called him Prince. The dog kept nearest him all the time, and it seemed to Joe as though he answered to his name.

When evening came, Joe spread a piece of old blanket for him on the porch, so that he had a bed. The collie lay down but did not stay there long. When Joe went up to his own bedroom, he looked out the window and saw Prince wandering around the grounds, searching for him. He looked lonely and forlorn out there in the moonlight.

Joe called to him. "Prince! Prince!"

The dog lifted his head and gave a low bark of delight. Then he went to the foot of the oak tree from where he got a full view of Joe's bedroom window. He lay down there with his head on his paws.

Joe watched him for a long time. Finally he went to bed; but a few minutes later he hopped out again to take just one more look.

Prince was still under the tree. He must have heard Joe, for he lifted his head, listening, watching, alert.

"Good boy, Prince," Joe called.

If only he could make this dog his own!

CHAPTER EIGHT

# *Farmer Wilson*

Joe awoke in the soft light of dawn, and his first thought was of the collie. He kicked back his sheet and blanket, jumped out of bed and looked out of the window.

There was Prince, under the tree just as last night. But surely he could not have been there all that time, Joe

107

thought. He must have gone hunting awhile in the long hours, and come back again. The collie was looking up, with his ears pricked to a point. He had no doubt heard him come to the window. And now as he caught sight of Joe, he got up and graciously waved his tail.

Joe listened for sounds in the big house, but all was silent. Everyone still seemed to be asleep. It was a nice feeling to be awake so early, just he and the dog.

He turned away and hurriedly washed and slipped into his shirt and jeans, and went downstairs. The dog and Joe met on the porch and sat down together on the top step. Joe put his arm around him and said, "Prince, Prince—that's your name now, so you'll have to get used to it."

Joe thought about Patch and Shaggy. He liked those dogs very much, but not like this collie. And they were dogs who could belong to almost anyone who was good to them. But this dog was different. He was serious and single-hearted. And he had chosen Joe.

The air smelled fresh and cool so early in the morning. Birds sang out from near-by trees, and from the deep, dense woods, in a chorus of joy.

Joe heard the cook coming downstairs, and a few other people stirring in the house behind him. He decided he would have a run with Prince. If he and the dog went off some distance from the house, where an occasional bark would not awaken sleepers at the Inn, it would be all right.

The sun came up over the eastern mountain ranges, flooding the world with its golden light. Joe got up, saying softly, "Come, Prince." And together they ran to the road and turned westward down the slope. The collie bounded about eagerly, then trotted ahead, leading the way. They ran to a place where the ground leveled out a little, before dipping on downward again. There was a brook down here with a small wooden bridge across it. They left the road and Joe untied and kicked off his sneakers, and he and the dog went splashing into the clear shallow water.

On the far bank among the scattered trees, a little distance away from the road, the collie found the smell of a woodchuck, and ran along, nose down, trying to trace it. But in a moment he came trotting back to Joe. Joe picked up dry sticks and threw them for Prince to chase. The dog dashed after them and brought them back.

Now the sun touched the high tops of the trees here on the shadowy slope of the mountain, crowning them with light. The first breakfast would be ready soon at the Inn. The cool morning and the romp had made Joe even hungrier than usual. So he got into his shoes and turned back to the house. Prince came instantly and trotted back with him.

Joe said to himself, "Prince is my dog. I can't ever give him up."

As he walked along, he tried to think out how he would word a letter to his father, explaining how important his friendship with the collie was, and asking permission to keep Prince if the owner did not show up. But he knew it was not going to be easy to write, for this was just what his father had asked him not to do.

Yet he felt that if his father could see this dog, he would understand how it was. After all, a boy has an obligation to an animal that has so great an affection for him. He tried again and again to put that into words, but he realized that to his father it would sound like another one of Joe's pleas for just any stray dog. He felt, helplessly, that writing would get him nowhere, and put it out of his mind.

The day turned into a lively one, for the Harveys, Linda and Bert and their parents, were going on a picnic and took Joe and Prince along. They drove to one of the high mountains some fifteen miles or so away, known for its magnificent view. They lunched on the mountainside and were back by mid-afternoon.

With this excursion, and with chores to do later, the day passed quickly for Joe. Now and then, all through the day, he had thought again that he should write his father and mother about the collie; and hopeless as it seemed, he decided he must try.

*Joe picked up dry sticks and threw them for Prince*

After supper he sat down at the table in his room and started.

"Dear Mom and Dad," he wrote, "I have found a dog up here that is the finest dog I ever knew. He is really a very unusual—"

No, that would not do, he knew. He started again, "I know you don't want me to get a dog for a while. But a collie has come here to the Inn who is the most wonderful dog I ever saw. Please let me have him."

No, that would not do, either. His parents would not understand, from these bare words, how very special the friendship between him and Prince was. How could he explain that?

He put the unfinished letters on the table by his bed, and wrote to Marty about Prince instead. That was much easier. He addressed and stamped the envelope, and then undressed to go to sleep. He would get Mrs. Carney to help him write to his parents tomorrow. He looked out of the window once more and saw that Prince was lying under the tree, his head on his paws, facing the window. He called to him, saying good night. Happy with Prince there, he climbed into bed and was soon asleep.

In the morning Joe again dashed to the window as soon as he awoke. He felt a little disappointed when he saw that Prince had gone away. But he reminded himself that dogs like to chase wild animals in the woods, and decided he had just not returned yet.

112

He went outdoors and called Prince. But still he did not come. That was strange. . . .

Joe went about the day's work and play with a troubled feeling. He kept wondering where Prince was. And when the dog did not come back by nightfall, nor all the next day, Joe became really very worried.

Mrs. Carney said, "Better put that nice dog out of your mind, Joe. It's just as well this way, because of your father and mother. They didn't want you to get hold of another stray dog anyway. You know that."

The Murrays, who had taken such a lively interest in Joe and his dog from the beginning, were almost as worried as Joe. Mrs. Murray said, "I don't think that dog is staying away because he wants to. I never saw such an attachment as that dog had for Joe."

"No, sir, he's not keeping away of his own free will," said Mr. Murray. "It doesn't add up."

The quiet Dr. Graham, who so seldom joined in the general conversation, left his chair and joined the others. "Most likely the dog's owner found him," he put in. "I just wonder whether he likes his owner as well as he likes Joe. Somehow, I doubt it. If there had been a real affection between him and his owner, he would not have been so exceptionally happy with Joe—not so soon, anyway."

Later that day, the Murrays went for a drive and did not return until nearly six-thirty in the evening. A number of the guests and Joe, too, were sitting on the porch, waiting for dinner, when they came walking around the house from the back, where they had parked their car.

Mrs. Murray, her usually gay face looking very gloomy, said, "Joe, we have news of your dog."

"You have?" asked Joe quickly.

"Not very good news," she said.

Mr. Murray put in, "One of the farmers down there in the valley—Wilson's his name—took out a license for your collie, Joe. He has him tied up behind his house. We saw him there."

Joe said, in a shocked voice, "No, not Prince, not my Prince?"

"I'm afraid so," said Mr. Murray, sitting down on the steps beside Joe.

Joe felt stricken. He knew the freedom-loving, proud young dog would hate being tied intensely. And, anyway, he was sure Prince wanted to be here with him, and not with the Wilsons or anyone else.

Joe blamed himself for his hesitancy in claiming Prince. He should have bought a license for him before any other person could. He should have done it just to protect the dog, while he tried to come to an understanding with his father.

"Tied up!" he said again. "That's awful. Prince couldn't stand being tied up long, not a dog like that."

There was a murmur of sympathy from the others along the porch.

114

Mrs. Murray said, "We asked Mr. Wilson if he would sell us the dog. But he wouldn't."

Mr. Murray, looking as downcast as though someone had done him a personal hurt, turned away and went into the house. Mrs. Murray started to follow, but stopped a moment in the doorway and turned back.

"Mr. Wilson said he was going to train the dog to herd the cows for him," she said. "That would be all right. But Mr. Wilson isn't gentle and affectionate with Prince. He's rough and iron-handed; and somehow I don't see that sweet-natured, dignified dog doing well with a man like that. He just isn't his kind." And then she, too, went into the house.

Joe sat miserably on the steps with this chin in his hands. He kept thinking about the dog, and how he loved him; and how awful the dog must feel, tied up there at Wilson's farm, not understanding why anyone would want to do that to him.

Joe had been aware vaguely that the gong had sounded for dinner and that the people on the porch had gone inside.

Then a voice behind him said, "Don't take it so hard, Joe." It was the doctor speaking. "Come in and have your dinner. The dog may get along all right with the farmer, and since you can't keep him, give it a chance."

Joe shook his head. He knew it was only said to comfort him. Then he looked up at the doctor and smiled. It was

115

not a smile of good cheer, but of appreciation for sympathy. The doctor knew how Joe felt; that was something.

The next few days, the life at the Inn went on much as usual for Joe. There was the great wide lawn to mow, and there was play with Linda and Bert. Some guests left on Friday, and an elderly couple arrived for their two weeks' vacation on Saturday. There were many diversions, but all the while the collie was in the back of Joe's thoughts, whatever went on about him. He knew that he had lost the chance to make him his dog, and he was sad all the time. He was ashamed, too, for he felt he had let the dog down.

After dark, some of the guests always took a little walk along the road. Joe usually went with them. There was something mysterious and wonderful about being out in the silence of the mountaintop at night, with no light but that of the stars in the vast arch of the sky.

One night at about nine o'clock, Joe was again walking along the road with several little groups of guests. Dr. Graham, the Murrays, and Linda and her mother and father were the nearest to Joe. Half a dozen other people were ahead of them, and a few trailed behind. Joe and his friends had turned the curve in the road, a sharp dip of the land had put the Inn abruptly out of sight. The strollers seemed small and lonely out there, with the trees and bushes black and silent on either side.

116

Linda was chattering. She was telling Joe about some of the things she did when she was at home in Cleveland. The voices of the grown people around them were low.

Suddenly something stirred in the brush, and a large creature sprang out and hurled itself at Joe. Joe staggered, and his heart thumped with surprise. Linda cried out, and so did a woman just behind them. The strollers all stopped to see what had leaped at Joe.

It was the collie!

Joe cried, "Prince, Prince!" The dog's paws were on his chest. He took them in his hands and set them down on the ground. "So you've come back to me, Prince. You've come back to me," he said.

The dog, wild with excitement that he had found Joe, kept throwing himself at the boy, almost knocking him over. Joe sat down in the grass and weeds at the side of the road and let the dog lick him and bump his nose against him, and get his fill of expressing his joy and relief.

Meanwhile, Joe's hands had discovered the rope around the dog's neck. It was knotted tightly and a short piece of it dragged along the ground. The end of it was frayed where the collie, after a long and tireless struggle, had torn or gnawed it off from the post or tree where he had been tied. Joe hated that rope, because he knew the dog hated it. His fingers set to work at the knot, but it was pulled so tight he could not undo it.

117

The people on the road had gathered around, and all were watching and exclaiming over Prince's return. They were so happy to see the dog and the boy together again.

Mr. Murray saw Joe working at the rope, and took a penknife out of his pocket. He said, "Here, Joe, let me cut that off."

In another minute the dog was free of the hated rope. Then again he excitedly walked all over Joe, as though he just could not get enough of him, could not get close enough to him.

At last, he quieted down and Joe said, "I guess I better take Prince home."

He and the dog turned back toward the Inn, and Linda, the Murrays and Doctor Graham went along. A few minutes later, by the back porch light, Joe began to work the brambles out of Prince's coat.

Mrs. Carney, who had been told by the Murrays what had happened, came out with a bowl of food for the dog. He ate it hungrily, almost ravenously.

Mrs. Carney said, "Those Wilsons! They never feed their dogs much. Expect them to live on wild creatures they hunt, rabbits and woodchucks and such. It's better for a dog to be fed regularly."

After a while, Joe and Mrs. Carney and some of the others discussed what could be done about the dog now. Could they get Mr. Wilson to give him up? And, if so, what could be done with Prince?

Mrs. Carney said they would keep the dog overnight, and telephone the farmer about him tomorrow. The dog would probably have to go back there.

"Anyway," she said, "let's think it over."

Joe didn't want to leave the dog outdoors overnight. "Let me keep him in my room just this one single night," he pleaded.

"No," said Mrs. Carney. "No dogs in the house."

The Murrays added their pleas to Joe's.

"Just tonight, please," Mrs. Murray said.

"Break your rule for us just this once," pleaded Mr. Murray. "We'll all sleep better knowing Prince is safely up there in Joe's room."

Mrs. Carney was not much pleased with the idea. She said, "I really don't like dogs in the house. But if it makes all of you happier—all right, just this once."

So Prince went upstairs with Joe. He slept on the small rug beside his bed, a contented dog.

## CHAPTER NINE

# *Big Dog in Trouble*

JOE was sitting at the small brown desk in the living room, with Prince beside him. It was never much fun to write, but he did want the boys to know about the collie and all that was happening to him. And, in turn, he wanted to hear from them, of course. Especially he wanted Phil to write to him about his adventures on the ranch. But even while he thought of this, it did not seem quite as important as his need to keep the collie, and the danger that he must give him up.

Mrs. Carney came into the room as he was finishing the second card. She cast a swift look at the dog, but said nothing for a while. She fussed around a little, raising a shade, fluffing out a window curtain. She seemed to have something on her mind; and after a few minutes she did speak.

"Joe, I've been thinking about this collie and you."

Joe turned around to her eagerly, and rested his chin on his hands on the chair back.

She went on, "Of course I can't help but remember that your father and mother asked you not to get a new dog now. What's more, they asked me to see that you didn't."

"Yes, I know," Joe said sadly. "If I just hadn't had so many other stray dogs to take care of this year, my father wouldn't have been so tired of it. He might have let me have a dog as super as Prince now, even if we do have to move in the autumn."

Mrs. Carney stood by the window, looking out over the lawn. And after a moment, she said, "Well, as it is, I couldn't let you have the collie, Joe. But, all the same, I won't let him go back to Mr. Wilson, either—if there's any way of stopping it. Prince isn't happy there, that's clear. I'll phone Mr. Wilson, and if he'll give Prince up, I'll keep the dog here myself, and you can get to work and find a home for him with someone he loves. Handle it for me, the way you did with the hound you gave the Jasons, or the way you did with Shaggy and Patch and Teddy."

"All right," said Joe, giving her a broad smile. She was swell. She even knew the names of all the dogs he had helped along. She was willing to claim Prince for his sake. If she did that, it would be next door to owning the dog himself. And, what's more, it would give Joe time. And if he had time, he could go on trying to get his parents' permission to keep the collie. He would write to-day for sure, he told himself.

Mrs. Carney said, "Come. I'm going to phone Mr. Wilson right now, and you can listen in. He's not such a bad sort of man, really. He's just stubborn and hasn't much sentiment about animals."

They went to the telephone in the hall, and Joe leaned close to the receiver. In a moment, Mr. Wilson was on the wire. Mrs. Carney explained that the stray collie he claimed was up at the Inn and asked him to give him to her. "The dog doesn't seem to take to you," she said. "You'll probably never be able to do anything with him, anyway. Certainly a dog you have to tie up isn't much good to you."

To this Mr. Wilson said that he had no intention of parting with the collie. "And if he runs away again," he said, "I'll beat it out of him."

"No, sir," said Mrs. Carney. "You don't beat him, or

I'll report you for cruelty to animals. This dog likes it up here and it's where he belongs. We'll even offer to buy him."

"Sure," Joe whispered to her. "I'll spend all the money I've earned this summer to get Prince."

Mr. Wilson did not hear Joe. He only heard what Mrs. Carney said, and he answered, "You can't have the dog, even for money. I'm going to train him. He'll be a good dog, once I get him trained."

"It may be more trouble than it's worth," said Mrs. Carney quietly.

But the farmer just said, "Hold the dog there for me. I'll drive up for him later."

"No, it's not up to me to keep him for you," Mrs. Carney said. "We'll turn him loose, and you can catch him where you find him." And she hung up.

"But, gosh," said Joe, "I can't really let Prince go away, Mrs. Carney. We'll feed him and try to keep him here, won't we? We can't let Mr. Wilson get hold of him and beat him."

"Oh, we'll feed him, all right. But we can't keep him against Mr. Wilson's will. The dog is legally his now because of the license," Mrs. Carney explained. But Joe knew she was on his and Prince's side, and that comforted him a little. She went on, "Anyway, where would the dog go? He'll stay right here, most likely, near you."

Mr. Wilson did not come up for the dog that day, and

123

everyone around the Inn was glad of that. But Joe kept watching for the farmer, because nothing really had been settled, and sooner or later he probably would come for the dog.

The next morning while Joe and Prince were in the vegetable garden, where Joe was picking string beans for Mrs. Carney, the dreaded moment came. Mr. Wilson's car swung up the road and into the Inn's driveway.

The farmer jumped out as soon as he brought the car to a stop. He looked pretty cross. And without saying anything to Joe, he whistled to Prince. The collie came toward him slowly, with his tail between his legs. Then he stopped, hesitating. The farmer went to Prince and put a rope around his neck. As he led him to his car, Prince pulled away, and looked back at Joe in a puzzled and sad way. But he was a gentle dog and did not struggle much. The farmer got into the car, pulled Prince in after him and closed the door. Then he said good-bye, stiffly, and drove away.

Two days later, the dog was back at the Inn. An early rising guest discovered him on the porch, with a torn length of rope around his neck, just as before.

When Joe saw him a little later, the dog's eyes looked sad and puzzled, as though he were asking Joe, "Why do you let the farmer take me away when you know I'm your dog? Why do you let him tie me up?" And Joe had a feeling of guilt toward the dog, and of failure—because

124

*Prince looked back at Joe in a puzzled and sad way*

he could not keep him and protect him. He again took the rope off as fast as he could, and then smoothed his fine coat and romped with him until he was happy again.

Prince and Joe stayed close together all that day, and Joe tried to make up to the collie for the unhappiness he had suffered while he was away. Everyone expected Mr. Wilson to telephone or drive up any moment, to claim the runaway. But the farmer again took his time about it. When nightfall came, the collie was still at the Inn with Joe.

Joe wanted to keep Prince in his room again that night, but Mrs. Carney would not let him this time.

She said, "As Mr. Wilson claims the dog, it's just as well not to do things that get Prince more and more attached to you, Joe. If he has to live with the farmer, the sooner he gets used to it, the better."

When Joe went to bed, the big young dog took his place under the oak tree in view of the bedroom window, as before. He seemed to be saying a long, affectionate good night. The grown-up summer guests were still out on the porch, and Joe lay in his bed, listening to the drone of their voices, for some minutes. He wondered where Prince would go on his hunting trip later that night. He was pretty sure now that Prince would not roam as far as the farm in the valley again, and with this comforting thought, he fell into a deep sleep.

Sometime later—it seemed far in the night—he was

126

aroused vaguely by the sound of knocking. For some time he was too wrapped in sleep to realize that the knocking was at his door. But then someone came into the room and took hold of his shoulder and gently shook him.

"Joe, wake up, Joe!" It was Dick, the young man who helped around the place. "Joe, wake up. Your dog's been hurt. Got in a fight with a porcupine."

Joe was instantly awake then. "What happened?" he asked, sitting up. He had only heard part of what Dick said.

Dick explained a little. "He got the porcupine quills in his mouth. That's what happened."

Joe did not stop to put on his shoes, and the two ran downstairs.

"I thought I ought to call you," Dick said on the way.

"Gee, yes," Joe said. "Thanks for waking me."

It was not really as late as Joe, aroused from a deep sleep, had thought. It was only about ten-thirty. Many of the guests were still up, and they were all out on the front lawn. They formed a circle about the dog, who was lying in the grass, in great pain. The doctor was there beside him, talking to him, trying to soothe him. The summer guests stepped back to make room for Joe and Dick.

"Joe," the doctor said, "this dog is in pretty bad shape."

"Prince!" Joe cried, shocked and horrified. He could

127

see the porcupine quills sticking through the collie's gums. It was a fearful sight. He knelt down beside him and stroked him. "Prince! Prince! We'll try to help you, Prince," he said, his voice choked with pity and grief.

"It's up to you to make a decision," the doctor told Joe. "When a dog is in as bad shape as this with porcupine quills, he's usually shot to put him out of his misery. But the way you and Prince like each other— well, I'll try to save his life, if you want me to."

"Taking out those quills will hurt badly," said Mrs. Carney.

"And we have no chloroform," Dick said. "Mrs. Carney looked for some, but there isn't any on hand."

"I want him saved—please," Joe said. "I'll never have him killed. Never."

"Okay," said Dr. Graham.

"Isn't there anything at all you can give Prince so it won't hurt him?" Joe asked, gulping down the tremor in his voice.

Mrs. Carney said, "No, there's nothing of that kind on hand. And the one drug store in the village is closed by now. We won't be able to get anything from there either."

"And this can't wait, Joe," the doctor said. "It has got to be done right away, if at all."

"Please save Prince," Joe said again. "Please, Dr. Graham, try to save him."

"All right, I will, Joe," said the doctor quietly. "And if it's any comfort to you to know it, I'm a surgeon. And I'll do the best operation on Prince I know how to do. Dick, here, can hold the dog. Will you, Dick? Joe loves him too much; it will be too tough on him to watch this."

"Sure," Dick said, "I'll hold the dog."

The doctor then called for what he needed. "Get me a pair of pliers from the tool shed, or from one of the cars. That's the best we can do at this hour. Boil them to sterilize them, and bring them out here to me. And we'll need a strong flashlight. The porch light won't do. It's too dim for me to work by."

Mrs. Carney and Dick went off; and Joe kept stroking the dog and talking to him. "You'll be all right soon, Prince. You won't hurt any more when we get you fixed up, fellow. You'll be all right."

The dog's pain-shot eyes looked at him, pleading for help.

Soon Dick came back with the sterilized pliers, and Mr. Murray appeared with a big flashlight and stood behind the doctor, fixing the beam on the dog's jowls.

"Better get back now, Joe," the doctor said.

Joe got up from the grass. But he could not bring himself to leave. He thought it might help Prince a little, give him a little confidence, if he stayed near by. He couldn't go off for his own comfort's sake and leave Prince alone in pain and fear. He stood beside the dog

129

with his head bowed, his hands up to his cheeks, ready to cover his eyes if need be.

The doctor began carefully and expertly to pull the first of the spiked quills from the dog's mouth. The dog whimpered and thrashed about. He tried to get up to run away.

Dick managed to hold him down forcefully. But as the next quill was pulled, he thrashed about so that he hurt himself all the more.

The doctor sucked in his breath in distress, and dropped the pliers. "I don't know," he said. "I don't think I'm going to be able to do this without an anesthetic. It's too much for the dog. He can't hold still enough."

Joe came forward into the small circle of light and knelt down by the collie.

"Wait," he said. "I think Prince will lie still better if I hold him."

"Maybe so," the doctor said with a sigh. "If you can bear it, Joe, why then come and take charge of Prince, and I'll try again."

Joe drew closer to the dog. He pressed his leg firmly along the length of his back, put one hand on his head, the other on his side. He did not hold him at all, just kept his hands on him affectionately and reassuringly. And the dog lay still.

The doctor pulled out another quill, and this time more swiftly and easily. The dog twitched, but then lay

130

quiet. Even when the pliers touched him again, he did not jerk away.

The doctor said, "I wouldn't believe it if I didn't see it. For love of Joe, the dog can stand all this pain."

There was a deep silence among the watchers as the doctor worked on. One after another the quills came out.

Most of the guests had turned away; some stood in a clump a little distance off in the darkness, waiting.

At last the doctor put the pliers down in the grass. "That's all," he said.

Joe sat still, talking softly to the dog, telling him that he would get well now, that the worst of the pain was over. One of his hands rested in the grass. And the dog lifted his torn jaws and laid them on Joe's hand. They stayed there like that for a long time.

Joe could hear the guests talking, relief in their voices. "That's wonderful, Doctor," one said. "I'm so glad you were here to save that dog," said another. "The way he loves Joe!" But Joe only heard this vaguely. He gave his full attention to comforting the collie. He was still afraid he might die.

The doctor spoke to Joe after a while. "Prince will be all right, Joe. He'll recover."

"Thanks," said Joe. Then, after a moment, he asked whether the doctor did not think the dog had better sleep upstairs that night.

"Joe, a sick dog is best off outside. Nature takes care

131

of animals. They know what to do for themselves out-doors. The earth is so clean up here on the mountains, and there are healing qualities in earth and plants. In-doors, he might just get infected. Better leave him here."

"All right," Joe said, and then, "Thank you for saving Prince's life, Doctor Graham."

"I'm glad I could do it," Dr. Graham said. "Come, let's get to bed."

Young Mrs. Murray came up to Joe. "Honey," she said, "I brought down an old sheet Mrs. Carney gave me. We've made a nice clean bed for Prince on the porch. See if he wants to lie on it."

Joe looked at Dr. Graham.

"Maybe the dog will feel more cared for there," the doctor said. "If he wants to, he can always come back out here and lie in the grass."

Joe nodded. Everyone was so wonderfully nice to Prince and him. He stood up and gently urged the dog to his feet. Prince got up weakly and came with Joe, walking slowly. He was a very sick dog. He came up on the porch and lay down on the soft, clean cloth that had been arranged for him.

Joe was all for spending the night right there beside Prince, sleeping on the boards of the porch with a cushion from a chair under his head. But Mrs. Carney was firmly against it. "What would your mother say if she heard I let you do that?" she asked.

So Joe went upstairs with the rest of the people. Mrs. Carney switched out the porch light, and only the hall light was left to spread its feeble glow. All was soon still in the Inn.

Joe slipped downstairs an hour or so later. He saw that the big dog was still lying quietly on the porch. Joe listened to the night sounds out of doors—the crickets' chirp; a single bird's lonely, drowsy note; then a small animal scampered along the hedge, a rabbit or a woodchuck, Joe guessed. It was a sound Prince usually loved. But now he lay still, too much in pain to care what went on about him. Joe prayed that Prince would get well.

CHAPTER TEN

# *A Deal Is Made*

Joe slept long the next morning, worn out with the strain of the previous night's happenings and with the late hours he had kept.

He hurried out to Prince as soon as he got downstairs, and found him lying under the drooping branches of the bushes at the back of the house. He thought of what Dr. Graham had said about the healing qualities of the clean earth. Dropping down beside Prince, he rolled over

134

on his stomach, and stuck his nose close against the soil. It smelled sweet and fragrant. The doctor was probably right, and Joe felt he need not worry about the dog's lying here.

But how sick he looked. All the vigor and the great joy that were so much a part of him had gone out of him like a light switched off. Joe stayed with him a little while, comforting him. And then he went in to get his breakfast.

Linda and Bert came and visited with him while he ate. They had slept uninterruptedly the night before and they wanted to hear over and over again how Prince was saved by the doctor. Finally they went off, after Joe had made them promise not to disturb Prince.

Joe was almost through with his breakfast when Dr. Graham and Mr. Murray came in. They said hello, and sat down at one end of the table, as though they were waiting for him. And a minute later, Mrs. Carney came in, too, and began to brush the crumbs from the table.

Joe took his plate and glass to the kitchen, and when he returned, Mr. Murray was saying, "I'm going to drive down and have a talk with that farmer who's taken out a license for Prince. Maybe Joe can't have this dog because his father hasn't been asked yet. But the first thing is to get the dog away from that place down there where he is so unhappy. The rest we can work out later."

"That's right," said Dr. Graham. "Mr. Murray, Mrs.

Carney and I will take the responsibility for this, Joe."

"Oh, gee, thanks," said Joe.

"Well," Mr. Murray said, "anyone coming with me?"

"Can I come?" Joe asked. And was assured that he could.

Dr. Graham said he had to be included; and to Joe's increasing surprise, even busy Mrs. Carney, who had always said she didn't care so very much about dogs, said she would join them.

"I wish you'd let me do the talking," she said to Mr. Murray. "I know Mr. Wilson from many years past, and I think I can handle him."

Mr. Murray nodded. "I'll be grateful to have you take over," he said.

"And don't any of you sound too eager to have the dog," she went on. "Mr. Wilson is not so apt to give Prince up if you do. He's a stubborn man."

She went upstairs to change into a neat navy blue dress. And Joe went in search of Linda and Bert, and asked them to keep an eye on Prince while he was away.

Then Joe's three grown-up friends came out and Joe got into Mr. Murray's car with them, and they drove off.

The long, winding mountain road dipped steadily downward for several miles. It was so narrow that it was like a slit cut through the thick woods. Sometimes the tall trees almost closed over their heads as they drove along. Sometimes they passed open, grassy places.

136

Rabbits darted along the edge of the road and disappeared into the weeds and bushes at the side. Crows called out raucously.

At last the land began to level out; they swung around in a long curve, passed a silo and a great red barn, and drew up before the Wilsons' white farmhouse.

Joe saw Mr. Wilson out at the shed, repairing some farm machinery. Aware that the car had stopped, the man wiped his hands on a piece of cloth and came toward them.

"Good morning," he said stiffly.

"Good morning," and "How do you do?" all in the car responded.

Mrs. Carney got out of the car, but then turned back to Joe for a moment. "Don't you say anything, Joe. You keep quiet. I can handle him best without you."

"All right," said Joe, and clenched his jaws firmly so he would not forget. He glanced at Dr. Graham and Mr. Murray, and they seemed to be doing that, too.

Mr. Wilson was standing beside the car with Mrs. Carney now. She said, "Mr. Wilson, I thought I'd better tell you—that collie, you know, well, he got into a fight with a porcupine last night. It's very bad. Want to come up to my place and take a look at him?"

Joe started to cry out, "No—," but Dr. Graham quickly put a hand on his knee and reminded him to keep quiet.

Mr. Wilson shook his head and said, "A porcupine?

137

Naw, I guess I won't come up. If it's bad, have someone shoot him, will you? That's about all one can do for a case of porcupine quills." His face didn't show much expression. He didn't care so very much one way or the other what happened to the collie.

"And if we tried to save him, and succeeded, we may keep him?" Mrs. Carney asked.

Mr. Wilson leaned on the car to think it over. "Well, no," he said after a moment. "If the dog can be saved, I'll naturally take him back."

Joe started to jump forward. He just had to put up a fight for his dog. But again the firm hand of the doctor reminded him to keep still, and gave him enough confidence to wait a moment more before he protested.

"Very well," Mrs. Carney was saying now. "We did save his life. Dr. Graham here took the quills out. If you want the dog back now you'll have to pay Dr. Graham's bill. It was a tough operation. His bill is thirty dollars, I understand."

"It's too much," said Mr. Wilson. "The whole dog ain't worth that much." He turned to Dr. Graham. "That's a pretty stiff price."

Dr. Graham got out of the car, looking thoughtful. "No, I don't think so," he said in his quiet, gentle way. "And if you had been there last night and had seen what I had to do to save that dog, you wouldn't either. Frankly, I ought to charge a lot more."

138

Mr. Wilson's face remained a blank, and he was silent for a long time. Joe leaned forward and grasped the car's window edge as he waited for the farmer's response.

Suddenly Mr. Wilson moved away from the car. "All right, keep the dog," he said to Dr. Graham.

"Thank you," Dr. Graham said, bowing his head slightly. He took his fountain pen from his jacket pocket, and fumbled through other pockets for a piece of paper but found none. Mr. Murray quickly handed him an envelope, and the doctor passed pen and paper to the farmer.

"Will you write on this that you're selling me the dog for the price of the unpaid bill?" Dr. Graham asked.

Mr. Wilson took pen and paper and began to write. He gave a little grunt. "I'm really glad to be rid of the beast," he said. "He's been nothing but trouble to me since the day I got him. And it cost me five dollars for the license, too."

"We'll pay you back for that," Dr. Graham assured him. "Then everything will be settled amicably, and no one will be any the worse off."

"If you'll do that," said Mr. Wilson, his face brightening a little, "I sure would be glad. I haven't any five dollars to throw away for nothing." He gave Dr. Graham the envelope on which he had written, as asked.

Joe felt himself relaxing, and his face began to spread

into a smile. He looked at Mr. Murray, who gave him a fine, vigorous wink, and then looked solemnly straight ahead again.

Dr. Graham gave Mr. Wilson a five-dollar bill, and Mrs. Carney said cheerfully, "Well, thank you, Mr. Wilson. I really think this will work out better for all of us."

She and the doctor got back into the car and, after brief good-byes, Mr. Murray drove them on toward the little town of Truley.

Joe was so happy he could not sit still. He told the doctor that he would pay him back the five dollars as soon as they got home. And Dr. Graham said he could do that, if he wanted to.

Joe thanked Mr. Murray, and Mrs. Carney, and the doctor over and over for what they had done for him and Prince.

"Don't thank me," said Mr. Murray. "I only drove the car."

"Don't thank me," said Dr. Graham. "I just helped Mrs. Carney make her deal."

"You don't have to thank me, either," said Mrs. Carney. "I just did the little I had to do about this so we can all have some peace at the Inn at last. And, anyway," she laughed, "I think all my summer guests would have walked out on me if we hadn't managed to get ownership of Prince, so that he can stay with Joe."

Joe said, "But Mrs. Carney, my father said. . . . I can't. . . ."

"Oh, I've already written your parents," Mrs. Carney said. "I sent them a letter several days ago by air mail. And I'll follow it up with another today. I'm asking them to let you keep the dog, because he's so exceptional with you. And if they disagree with me about that, I'll consider him Dr. Graham's and Mr. Murray's and mine, till we can find him a home where he'll be happy. It won't take long to get your parents' answer. We could hear in less than a week by air mail."

The days passed and the collie's wounds began to heal. The doctor looked Prince over every day; and always he told Joe, "The patient is doing well. He's making a fine recovery. Just a few more days and he'll be himself again."

The first part of the week Prince was very quiet, and most of the time he stayed close around the Inn, but sometimes he went off to the woods for some hours. And once when Joe went in search of him, he found him lying in a cool, shadowy place near the brook, his fevered jaws on the damp earth. Joe sat on a rock and watched him, and listened to the chatter of the brook as it flowed over the rocks and stones.

And every day when Dick brought the mail up from Truley, Joe hoped for a letter from his parents. He was

141

pretty sure his mother would give in about Prince. It was only his father that he was worried about.

At last one day a letter from Dad came from France. It was addressed to Mrs. Carney, and said, "So there *are* stray dogs for Joe, even on lonely mountaintops! Well, if you really feel this is so important, I'll give my permission for Joe to keep the collie. But I do it rather regretfully. I do think it would have been better for Joe to have proved to himself and to us that he can leave dogs alone when there's a good reason for it. As a matter of fact, the reason for it is about gone, for I have been informed that I am not to take up the atomic energy research for the Government for the present. And so, as we are going to stay on in Brewster Hills, it really will be quite all right about the dog."

It was not a very satisfying letter, because of Dr. Collins' half-hearted consent. But at least the dog was Joe's now—really his. And as Prince's wounds had healed, and he completely recovered, he and Joe had a great time together for the rest of the summer.

Prince wore a collar with his license attached to it, and another tag, which the Murrays got for him. It bore Prince's name, and that of his owner, Joe Collins. Sky Inn was engraved on one side, as it was his summer address, and Brewster Hills, his winter address, was on the other side.

The summer was drawing to its close. The Murrays

*Joe found him . . . his fevered jaws on the damp earth*

left one Sunday afternoon; and by the next week end Dr. Graham, too, was gone. Then another letter came from Dr. and Mrs. Collins. This time they wrote that they would be on board a steamer crossing the Atlantic in a few days, and would be home the twentieth of August. They wanted Joe to come back to Brewster Hills soon after that, for they were eager to see him. They had been separated so long.

So Mrs. Carney and Joe began to plan for Joe's trip home with Prince.

As Joe packed his things a few days later, he thought again and again about his Dad's coolness to dogs, and hoped he would be at least a little friendly to Prince. The collie was sensitive and would not be fully happy if he were not liked by all the family.

Joe thought, "If Dad doesn't like Prince, I'll just have to keep my dog out of his way as much as possible. We'll manage somehow."

CHAPTER ELEVEN

# *Back in Brewster Hills*

THE train on which Joe was coming home pulled into the Brewster Hills station and came to a stop with a pleasant rush of steam and the clang of iron against iron. A trainman opened the door of the baggage car, where Joe was riding with Prince.

Joe hopped out, and the collie followed him and stood looking about him, his head up, his ears erect with interest in this new place.

Far off at the other end of the station platform, Joe

145

saw his mother and father and Marty. They were watching the few people who were coming out of the passenger cars, and looking puzzled because Joe was not among them. Joe, with Prince on his leash and carrying his heavy suitcase, hurried toward them. He had almost reached them before they saw him.

Then Marty called, "Oh, look! There he is!"

"Joe!" cried Mrs. Collins. "Back there?"

"We should have thought to look toward the baggage car," Dr. Collins said dryly. "He was riding with the collie, of course."

Mrs. Collins reached Joe first, and kissed him. "How you've grown, dear, in just these two months!" she cried.

Then Dr. Collins and Marty were beside him, too, and they were all talking about how good it was to be together again.

Marty and Mrs. Collins admired the collie, and exclaimed how beautiful he was. Even Dr. Collins agreed that he was certainly a fine, handsome animal.

Prince stood quietly by, wondering about all these new people, and sensing their importance to Joe. Yet he kept a certain aloofness because they were, after all, still strangers to him. And he waved his silken tail just a little as they petted him.

The Collinses drove off, Marty, Joe and Prince riding together in the back seat. Everybody talked of the summer's happenings.

146

Arriving at home, the family piled out of the car and went into the house by the front door. Prince stood aside, waiting to see if he would be asked in.

"Come in, for goodness' sake," Dr. Collins said gruffly to the dog.

Joe, too, urged him, putting his hand on his collar and talking to him. Then he explained to his father, "He isn't used to coming indoors much. Up at the Inn he stayed outdoors almost all the time."

"And anyway, Dad," Marty said, "you usually don't like dogs in the house. A smart, sensitive dog like this probably feels that."

Dr. Collins said, "Well, I don't want this dog indoors all the time, either. But at least he can come in now and look the place over, if it's going to be his home."

Mrs. Collins flashed a quick smile at Joe which seemed to say, "It looks as though your father likes this dog." And Joe smiled back, feeling relieved.

Inside the house, Prince kept close to Joe. He ran upstairs with him when the boy took his bag up. He sniffed along the hall and in the bedroom, while Joe washed and brushed his hair. He trotted back down with him when Mrs. Collins called Joe to come and have a bite to eat.

Joe had had lunch on the train—some sandwiches and ice cream—but he was hungry again, and hurried to the dining room. His parents and Marty came in and out of the room to talk to him while he ate. When he had finished, he and his sister and Prince went outdoors and looked the grounds over. After a while, Joe asked Marty to tell his mother he was going around the neighborhood to see some of the boys and girls he knew, and to show them his dog.

He did not put a leash on Prince now, as he had always done with Patch and Shaggy. Prince would never stray from him, he knew.

He went to the Applebys' first, to see if Phil had arrived from the West. He knew his friend would be staying there until his mother closed Sky Inn and opened their home here. Joe found Grandpa Appleby on the terrace, and talked to him. But, no, he was told, his friend had not arrived yet. Teddy, the Applebys' boxer, wasn't home either at the moment, so Joe could not introduce the two dogs to each other.

"Expect Phil tomorrow," Grandpa Appleby told Joe, and then added, "Nice collie you have there. Giving him away, like you did the others at the beginning of summer?"

"No, sir," answered Joe, "not this dog. He's mine to keep."

Joe went on to see Dan then, and found him at home, as well as Betsy. They had a grand reunion. Dan and his dog took to the collie immediately.

Betsy pranced around Prince, and the collie lifted a

paw and playfully pushed at the smaller dog. A game was on. Around and around the lawn they ran, now and then tumbling over in the grass, and harmlessly biting at each other for the fun of it.

"They're going to be pals," Dan said.

"I just knew they would," cried Joe.

The boys stood grinning happily as they watched, feeling that their own friendship was knitted more closely by the way the dogs liked each other. Finally they sat down on the steps and talked of the summer's happenings. Dan told of the fun he had had on his uncle's farm. Joe told about Prince's coming to Sky Inn, of how he got hurt trying to catch the porcupine, and of how Dr. Graham saved his life.

After a while, Joe got up. He had to look in on some of his other friends, he told Dan. "Make the rounds."

"Be seeing you," Dan said.

"Sure. Tomorrow," Joe said, as he and Prince went away.

Approaching the Averys' house, Joe called out, "Shaggy, hey Shaggy!" And in a moment the little gray and white dog came racing down the front walk to Joe. But then she saw the big collie and caution took the upper hand. She stopped abruptly, and stood staring at Prince, then turned about and scampered back to the house and safety.

Joe laughed. "Is Prince too big for you, Shaggy?" he

149

asked. "He won't hurt you. And you'll have to get used to him."

He went in and had a short visit with Mrs. Avery and little Sue. He tried to get Shaggy to become friendly with Prince, who looked interested. But Shaggy was still shy and cautious. That would break down gradually, though, Joe felt certain.

After a few minutes more, Joe went on to see Mary Lou Denis. Mary Lou was on the sidewalk in front of the house and came skipping to meet Joe when she saw him.

"Oh, Joe, when did you get home? And where did you get that collie?" she asked all in one breath.

And again he had to tell something of the way he and the collie had come together.

"And how are old Patch and your cat getting along?" Joe wanted to know.

"Chums!" Mary Lou said. "They're real chums now. Come and see them." She looked at Prince. "We'd better put Prince in the house while we go to look at them. They're in the back yard. Prince is new to them, and he would wake them up. But if you come alone on tiptoe, you can see what I want you to see."

So they put Prince in the living room, and left him there for Mrs. Denis to admire; and then went through the kitchen and tiptoed out the back door.

There, close to the house on the cool earth of a flower

150

*"They're going to be pals," Dan said*

border, lay Patch, and—amazing sight—the cat, small, rakish Mike—lay practically in his arms. His head was actually pillowed on one of Patch's outstretched fore-legs.

"Gosh!" Joe said. "And we worried over them once! We wondered whether Patch would ever get used to any cat!"

Patch awoke at the sound of Joe's voice and jumped up to greet him. He spilled Mike over into the grass in his hurry; but Mike did not mind. He sat up, yawned, and went off by himself, walking as softly as down drift-ing across the grass.

Joe romped with Patch, and then called Prince. The collie came trotting through the house and nosed the back screen door. Joe let him out to meet Patch, and the two dogs sniffed at each other by way of getting acquainted. They held themselves a little tense at first, but then began to run around together excitedly. Joe watched this a while and then hitched up his slacks, ready to be on his way. He said good-bye to the Denises and went off toward Canfield Road.

It was great to be back in Brewster Hills and see all his friends, two-legged and four-footed.

That evening after supper Joe brought Prince in from the yard and put him on the back porch where his other dogs had always slept. Then he went into the living room to be with his family.

Father and Mother had a lot of snapshots to show Marty and Joe, pictures they took in Europe. They all sat down on the davenport together to look at them. Dr. Collins lit his pipe, and then, with the pictures in hand, looked around the room, as if searching for someone.

"Where's Prince?" he asked.

"On the porch," Joe answered. "Shall I let him come in with us?"

Mrs. Collins and Marty were in favor of it. But Dr. Collins said, "I just wanted to make sure he was home and not straying around the town. But let him in for a moment if you like."

Joe popped up like a firecracker, and was back in a moment with Prince. The dog came to each of them to be petted. He had the family's whole attention, and as this went on for several minutes, Dr. Collins grew impatient.

"Are we going to look at these pictures, or aren't we?" he asked.

Joe and Marty of course said quickly that they certainly did want to see them. And Dr. Collins suggested that Joe had better take the dog to the back porch then.

Joe led Prince away, but he was disappointed. When his father had asked for the dog, Joe had hoped he was beginning to like him as much as anyone in the family

153

did. But clearly that was not so. Prince looked disappointed, too. He would have liked to stay with the family all evening.

Back in the living room, Joe sat on the davenport beside Marty. Mother and Father showed them the pictures and told them about all these places they had seen in France. It was a good evening and the family stayed up a little longer than usual.

As Joe went to bed that night, he heard a dog barking some distance away. It sounded lonely in the night. It might be a lost dog. He wondered then whether he would really have to give up collecting strays entirely now. Would he be able to, even if someone telephoned him to ask his help, as the grocer, Mr. Parker, had done last June?

He decided that he must. His father had given in about keeping Prince. In turn, Joe knew he would have to stop bringing new lost dogs into the house every few months. Father never did and never would like it, and he had a right to have his wishes considered. But the decision made Joe feel very sad: many a lost dog of Brewster Hills would have a hard time because of it in the years ahead.

The next day Joe and Prince again made the rounds, visiting the neighborhood, and for a while Joe played ball with some of the boys. In the afternoon, Phil arrived at the Applebys', and then came looking for Joe and Dan. And now there was more talk, this time largely about the cattle country of the West, where Phil had had such a fine time.

Next, Mrs. Carney returned from Sky Inn, which she had closed up for the season. A few more days, and school opened. And there were more boys and girls whom Joe could tell about Prince; more who came home with him to see his dog and admire him. The Jasons, Tom, Charlotte and Ellen, were among them. The Jason children came down from the farm every day to go to school; usually their father or mother drove them in, but in good weather they sometimes walked home again at three. So Joe saw a lot of them.

One day at recess, Tom asked Joe to come out to the farm on a Saturday and spend the day.

"And bring Prince," he said.

Joe was eager to accept the invitation, and began to plan for that day in the country. But for several weeks it rained on Saturdays, and once Mrs. Collins took Joe up to the near-by big city with her to buy him a new suit. And so it was some time before he was able to go to the farm.

CHAPTER TWELVE

# Visiting the Jasons

AUTUMN came early and brilliantly to Brewster Hills that year. By mid-October the trees around the town, and all the wooded mountains to the northwest, were a bright red and gold and rose. But then a heavy frost came one night, and the glory of color dulled and turned to brown.

Toward the end of the month, just a few days before October turned into November, Dr. and Mrs. Collins were going to the near-by big city one Saturday. Dr.

Collins was due at the Science Institute, and Mrs. Collins wanted to do some shopping. Then in the evening they were to have dinner with friends. They were going to make a day of it; and would be home on the ten-five train that night in all likelihood.

Joe and Marty had arranged their day to fit in with their parents' plans. Marty would go to her best friend Dotty's house for supper. But she would be home around nine, so that she would be there with Joe when bedtime came.

As for Joe, he had chosen this day for his visit to the Jasons' farm in the long valley between the hills. He could hardly wait to get started. And Prince, sensing that Joe was about to set out on some expedition, trailed after him through the house, looking at him with eager, questioning eyes. He wanted to make sure that whatever Joe was about to do, he, Prince, would get to go along.

"Sure you're coming with me, Prince," Joe told the collie, to put him at ease.

The Jasons had asked Dan and his dog Betsy to come out, too. Joe would have liked their company for the walk, but Dan and his mother had gone to visit relatives in a near-by town for the week end, and Betsy had been left in a neighbor's care.

Joe made himself a lunch to take along. He made some sandwiches, and put them, together with an orange and

157

a chocolate bar, into a paper bag. He would eat whenever he got hungry on the way. He wore corduroy slacks and a light, short jacket that cut the wind well and zipped up to the neck. He did not want to be too heavily dressed for so long a walk.

"Be sure and get back before dark, Joe," his mother said, "unless someone is going to drive you home."

"If I do get a ride back, can I stay at the Jasons' for supper?" Joe asked.

"Why, yes," Mother said. "But if you have to walk, better leave there a little before four. It gets dark early now, and you should be home by five o'clock. You can get your own supper here, then. There's lots of food in the refrigerator for you. There's a pot roast you can cut some slices from; and be sure to heat up the broccoli left from last night. You'll want a vegetable. And then there's apple sauce for your dessert."

"All right," said Joe cheerfully. He liked an opportunity to eat whatever he wanted out of the refrigerator, all by himself.

He and Prince left the house a few minutes later, a little before his parents had to start to the station for their train. The dry leaves rustled under their feet as boy and dog went along. The air was crisp, but the sunshine was warm. Beyond the last trees of the town, the road cut through the meadow. Joe looked for late purple asters and goldenrod, but he saw that the recent frost had taken

158

the life out of all of them. They stood faded and ready for winter.

Prince was enjoying the walk tremendously. He trotted along briskly, sometimes getting far ahead and then racing back to Joe. He dashed into the weeds every now and then, trailing the scent of a woodchuck or chasing a rabbit.

Now the road turned in between the low mountains, and a mile and a half farther on the land flattened out broadly. Cows grazed in the pasture; and there were bare fields where hay and corn had grown in the summer. A low, sparsely wooded hill, rocky and broad at the base, lay on the right. Joe and Prince had to circle this before they would reach the first farmhouse, where an elderly couple lived. And there was another mile to go beyond, before they would reach the Jasons' farm.

Joe was impatient to be there, and thought of climbing over the eastern slope of the wooded hill to make a short cut. But he decided against it, because he was not really in a hurry at all, and the valley was pleasant in the mid-day sunshine.

Joe thought, "If the road had just been put on the other side of the hill, the trip to the Jasons' would be about three-quarters of a mile shorter."

He decided to eat his lunch now. So he sat down on a big flat rock near the road and bit into a sandwich. Prince got a few bites of everything, including a slice of the orange. Lunch finished, Joe and Prince went on along the curving, sunny road, and at last came to the Jasons' place.

The hound Rambler was the first to see them. He barked loudly, because Prince was new to him. Joe called to Rambler, and put his hand on Prince's back, so that Rambler would understand and accept Prince as a friend. The hound came up to them, his very long ears flopping, his sad eyes intent on the new dog. He and Prince sniffed at each other.

Tom, Ellen and Charlotte Jason, who had been waiting for Joe, came out of the house. Tom wore a new red plaid shirt, and the girls were in brown skirts and blue sweaters. The Jasons and Joe greeted each other with "hellos" and "hi-yas."

Tom wanted Joe to come and see the two turkeys his father had bought recently, and was fattening up for Thanksgiving. Ellen and Charlotte asked why Marty had not come along, and Joe explained that there was no one to drive them out, and Marty was too lazy to come on such a long walk.

The two dogs were friends now, and trotted off, sniffing the ground and stopping once in a while to play with each other.

The boys and girls went on to the farmyard, and there Joe saw the turkeys, the great gawky birds, with the curious flaps and rolls and sacks of skin around their faces and under their necks.

160

"Funny-looking from close by, aren't they?" Tom said.

"They sure are," Joe agreed.

"I'm scared of them," Ellen explained to Joe, standing well back from the fence.

"That's silly," said her older sister.

Mrs. Jason called from the back door, "Hello, Joe. Glad to see you. Don't you want some lunch?"

"No, thank you. I've had mine," Joe called back.

Charlotte said to Joe, "Come and see the newest calf, Joe. It's two months old now, and pretty big."

"A nice little calf," said Tom. "You haven't been out for ages, Joe, so you haven't seen any of this year's calves."

"That's right," Joe said, and reminded them that the reason he had not been out to visit them all summer was because he had been up at Sky Inn so long.

They went around behind the barn, and down a dip in the ground where a tiny brook trickled. As they crossed, Joe said, "The brook is low."

Tom explained that there had not been enough rain lately. "But the weather report over the radio said maybe there will be a little rain late tonight, and it's going to get colder. Maybe freeze," he said.

And it was true that there was a growing chilliness in the air.

"It's already getting colder now," Ellen said. "I'm shivering. It's going to be winter soon."

They came into the pasture where the cows were, and

161

went among them. They were all tame and stood still while Joe patted them and rubbed their soft noses.

After a while, the girls and Tom and Joe went to the barn where the swings were. Joe thought swinging just a little sissy for a fellow twelve and a half. But after he and Tom had swung the girls, they took their turn at it, too.

Next they went indoors. Mr. Jason, who had come in after repairing a fence between the cow pasture and a field, was resting a moment, listening to the radio and smoking his pipe.

"How are you going back to town tonight?" he asked Joe. "Found anyone to drive you?"

"No, I'm walking home," said Joe.

"Well, I tell you, Joe," Mrs. Jason said, "my cousin, Bryson Smith, and his wife, they're driving in to Brewster Hills tonight to go to the movies. They live up yonder, you know, ten miles farther on. You could drive back with them."

"Yes," Charlotte said, "drive in with them, Joe. Then you can stay later."

"Sure I will," Joe said, "if the Smiths will take me along."

"Of course they will," said Mrs. Jason. "I'll telephone them and ask them to stop by here for you." So she did that, and came to report that all was arranged, and Joe should stay for supper. Then the boys and girls went on

162

*They were all tame and stood still while Joe patted them
and rubbed their soft noses*

about the place, looking at farm machinery, playing, and doing odd jobs.

A little after four, in the slanting light of the autumn evening, the cows began to come in toward the barn, knowing that it was milking and feeding time. Tom and Joe, with the two dogs, went out to open the gate and let the cows into the barnyard.

Shortly afterward, when Tom was helping his father get the milking machine ready to use, Mrs. Jason came out of the house and hurried toward the barn.

"Joe," she called, standing by the barnyard gate, "those cousins of ours, the Smiths, just phoned. One of their children is sick, so they can't go to town tonight, after all. You'd better get started for home quickly."

"Gee, yes," said Joe.

"I'll drive you in if you want me to, Joe," said Mr. Jason. "But I think you can make it all right before it gets really dark."

Joe could hear in his voice that Mr. Jason was tired and did not very much want to drive in to Brewster Hills after his day's work.

"Oh, yes, I can get home all right," said Joe. "I'll start now."

He and Tom and Mrs. Jason said good-bye to each other, and Joe hurried back to the house with Mrs. Jason. Prince came and walked at his side. At the house were Ellen and Charlotte, and they talked to Joe as he got

164

ready to leave.

Mrs. Jason said, "You ought to phone your sister, Joe, and tell her you'll be late."

Joe decided that he would. Marty probably would be at Dotty's by now. But suppose she didn't go over till dinnertime—then she'd miss him and worry. He picked up the receiver, but nothing happened; the Jasons' line was evidently out of order. So he gave it up.

He drank a glass of milk, and took the large sandwich of bread and ham which Mrs. Jason gave him to eat on the way home. He said good-bye to her and the girls, and then from outside on the road he called a loud good-bye to Tom and Mr. Jason once more. His voice echoed against the mountain to the south, and delighting in the sound, he repeated it just for fun.

Then he and Prince started out at a good fast pace. The sky had become overcast, and evening gray came on more quickly. Joe wished he and Prince could hitchhike home. He looked up and down the lonely country road for a car as he hurried along. But there was none anywhere in sight. It was a little after five o'clock by now, and real darkness would be setting in shortly.

Before very long he and Prince came to the broad, rocky hill again. Joe thought of the long walk he would be saved if he could cut across the southeastern slope of the hill. He considered the matter for a moment and decided to do it. He had always wanted to try it, anyway,

165

and now that he was in a hurry, it seemed a good time to do it.

He left the road and struck into woods along the lower edge of the hill. Prince was delighted. He sniffed the ground and trotted here and there round about Joe. At first the land, though rough, was at least open, and they followed what looked like a trail, but pretty soon this spread out into a half dozen faint trails going off in several directions.

Prince stayed nearer Joe than usual now, excited, alert. And Joe thought, "He knows this is unfamiliar ground to me."

Now they came into thicker woods with taller trees. And because they were climbing uphill and over rocky ground, they were not making as much speed as Joe had expected. He began to wish he had not taken the short cut. It was growing colder, too, and his corduroy pants and windbreaker did not feel very snug.

However, he kept fairly warm by climbing hard. But it was growing darker moment by moment, and the fact that they were on the east side of the hill, away from the pale light of the western sky, made the darkness still deeper.

Now he and Prince were over the ridge of the hill and Joe thought he should be able to see the road from here. But there were too many trees. And suddenly he had a fearful feeling that he was uncertain of his directions.

166

His face and hands felt cold, and he thought, "It really is going to be freezing weather tonight, like Tom said."

He talked to Prince. It made him feel good to have the dog close beside him. They came suddenly upon an abrupt gully, about fifteen feet deep. There was no way of crossing here, for this side of the gully was as sharply cut as a cliff. The darkness made it even more dangerous to climb down. He must search for a lower or more gradual slope. He would be delayed, but there was nothing else to do.

Prince looked up at Joe, waiting for his decision. Joe said, "This is tough, Prince. We're going to get home awful late." And Prince answered with a low half-bark that seemed to say that he too was a little worried about the gully, and impatient to get home.

"What'll we do now?" Joe asked. He looked up the gully to the northwest, and then down in the other direction. Somewhere, not too far off, there must be a better way to cross.

## CHAPTER THIRTEEN

# *Unfamiliar Way Home*

A LIGHT, icy rain had begun to fall, and Joe shivered a little. He and Prince walked up and down along the edge of the gully, looking for a place to climb down. But

168

wherever he looked, the wall remained very steep.

Joe was becoming aware that he was hungry. He took the sandwich Mrs. Jason had given him from his pocket, gave Prince his share, and ate the rest as he walked along. When he had finished, he decided he would have to climb down the gully here where he stood, even though the going did not look very easy. There was no better place anywhere in sight, and he did not want to lose more time in hunting.

It was just this bank that was so steep; the other side sloped much more gently. So, once he got down to the bottom of the gully, the most difficult part of the crossing would be over. He was the more eager to cross here because, if he wandered on, he might lose his direction completely. The gully made many twists and turns, and that, together with the increasing darkness, would add to the confusion he already felt. Actually, he told himself, he was not sure at this moment just which way the road lay. And he must strike into it again somewhere to the north.

He was much later already than he should be—it was long past the time he had told his mother and father he would be home. Marty would probably not miss him until even later, though, when she came home from Dotty's house. And Mother and Father would not be home yet, Joe knew; still he had a feeling of urgency about keeping his promise to them, and at least wanted to get back as

169

soon as possible. Besides, he was most eager to get out of the cold rain and the darkness.

He knelt at the edge and examined the wall of the gully closely. His hand, touching the ground, felt ice crystals forming where the rain had fallen. He found a spot in the wall which, though abrupt, offered some footholds in the rocks.

"Okay, Prince," he said, and started down. He held to a shrub while he felt around for a place to set his foot.

Prince stood watching Joe, and did not approve of what he was doing. He trembled with nervousness, and whimpered briefly. Joe knew that, aside from worrying about him, the dog did not feel sure that he himself could climb down at this point. But seeing that Joe was determined on the descent, Prince trotted quickly back and forth, looking for a place of his own choice.

Joe knew that dogs have a good sense of direction, and that, even should Prince go quite far along the gully before he crossed, he would get back to him in a few minutes.

He reached for another foothold, and in doing so his full weight hung on the shrub to which he was holding. Its roots abruptly pulled out of the thin, wet soil, and Joe tumbled backward and fell with full force on the rocks twelve feet or more below.

He cried out in pain, and Prince ran back toward him, and stood in unhappy uncertainty for just a second at the

170

top of the rocky wall.

Joe tried to get up, but could not. There was a terrible pain in his left leg, a pain such as he had never felt before. And when he put his hand where it hurt most he could feel the bone thrown out of its natural line. He knew then that it was broken, and badly.

Prince had held back only a moment. Now he raced a little distance away, found a place he could risk and made the descent into the gully rapidly, sliding part of the way with loose rock and earth. But he did not get hurt. He ran to Joe's side, stuck his nose against his face in loving concern, and then sniffed him anxiously here and there, knowing he was hurt.

"We've got to get out of here, Prince," Joe said in fright and pain. He tried again to pull himself up, but sank back with a groan.

Rain and night and ice were settling down on the earth. Joe was unable to move; and no one knew where he was, or even that he was in trouble.

Prince was frantic; he stepped around Joe, bumping him gently with his nose, again and again, and making a whimpering sound. He was trying to urge his dearly loved friend to his feet. He knew he must get him out of there somehow.

Joe kept saying, "Prince, I can't get up. My leg's broken. I can't get up. Gosh, I'm glad I've got you with me, Prince!"

He thought, "I wonder when Marty will get home and miss me? She'll wait a while, and then if I still don't show up, she'll try to phone the Jasons. But the line is out of order. Maybe she'll guess that something has happened to me. And after a while maybe she'll get someone to come out with her to hunt for me. Gosh, I hope someone comes soon."

Joe was half-lying, half-sitting, and his leg hurt badly. He stretched out and lay flat and felt a little better. He pushed his back against the big rock which had caused his injury. He was cold, and the rock gave him a very small bit of protection from the fine drizzle of icy rain. He could barely see his wrist watch, but he must be reading it right when it seemed to show a few minutes to six o'clock. He settled down for a long wait, cold and in pain.

Seeing Joe give up like this, the collie grew more and more alarmed. He kept nosing him, and finally he had an idea. If he could not get Joe home, he could at least give him warmth, and so keep him safe. He lay down close against him, and Joe put his arms around the big collie and relaxed in some relief. The dog was wonderfully warm.

They lay close together there for some time. The minutes dragged by. Joe drowsed, but awoke again because of the pain in his leg.

The collie was growing increasingly restless. He seemed to know that this waiting was not getting them

172

anywhere; that his beloved Joe was still in pain and in serious danger.

He got up, sniffed the place he had left, and seemed to take some satisfaction in the warmth he had given Joe. He stood back, uncertain for a moment, then suddenly seemed to make up his mind as to what he would do.

He gave Joe a quick lick on the cheek and then trotted off down the gully. He looked back once, and disappeared around a bend.

Joe's fright arose anew when he was all alone. But he told himself that whatever Prince had in mind, he would surely be back.

Not many minutes later he heard his collie barking from what seemed a long distance away. Perhaps he was calling for help down at the road, Joe thought in hope.

Then the barking stopped, and Joe lay wondering what his dog was doing now. Before long Prince reappeared. He came from the opposite side of the gully, walked carefully down the more gently sloping embankment there, and hurried over to Joe.

"Hi, Prince," Joe murmured, relieved to have him back. But he added in a shaky voice, "I guess you didn't find anybody to help us." It made him feel better, though, to talk to Prince, even if the dog could not fully understand. Joe's teeth chattered. Prince lay down against him once more, carefully and without hurting Joe's leg. Joe relaxed a little in the warmth of his body. He buried his hands in the collie's long, silky hair.

"You're swell, Prince," he said softly. "I don't know what I'd do without you." And the dog looked at him with his fine head raised, his eyes worried and full of longing to help.

After Prince had warmed Joe for a while, he got up once more, and trotted off. He looked back at Joe in distress, from time to time, until he was out of sight.

This time he was gone a very long time. Joe thought about his father and mother and Marty and wondered whether they were home by now and had missed him. He tried to see what time it was again, but it was so dark now that he could not. He thought it must be near nine o'clock. And he was so cold, and his leg hurt so badly, that he thought he could not bear it much longer.

The time dragged terribly with Prince away. Joe fought against being afraid, and put his mind on his family. He knew they loved him and would look for him in time.

At last he heard the barking of several dogs on the distant road. Then silence again, and a few minutes later, soft, light sounds in the woods. He thought that might be Prince coming back.

So it was, but he was not alone. This time he had Dan's Betsy and the Averys' Shaggy with him! How wonderful of them all, Joe thought.

"Prince!" he cried. "You brought me Betsy and

174

Shaggy! You're the most wonderful dog anyone ever had."

The dogs climbed down the east bank with fair ease and came scampering to him. They walked around him, sniffing him, backing away a little and giving excited, worried little yaps. How eager and earnest all three of them looked.

Joe reached out and patted them. They felt wet, and tiny particles of ice clung to their hair. His own jacket crackled with lightly crusting ice, too, as he moved.

Prince must have gone all the way into the town for help, Joe thought, and not being able to get any human beings to understand him, he had brought the dogs.

Prince had been very smart to bring Betsy and Shaggy, Joe soon realized. For now he and Shaggy stayed with Joe while Betsy went off to bark for help. Shaggy lay against Joe's neck, and Prince gently against his legs and stomach.

Joe watched Betsy race off, and soon he and Prince and Shaggy could hear her bark. She must be on the road then. She barked urgently, uninterruptedly, for a long time.

Joe thought there must be some cars passing, once in a while. But doubtless the people in them did not understand what the dog was barking for, and simply drove on.

Joe wondered whether anyone ever would understand and come to help him. He thought of the possibility of

175

dragging himself slowly out toward the road. The dogs had found the way, and they could lead him to it. But then he looked about him and knew he could never pull himself out of this gully and through the woods, with his broken leg hurting so.

At length Betsy came back. Then Prince got up and trotted off, and Betsy lay down in his place and helped keep Joe warm. Shaggy trotted a little way after Prince, but seemed to decide that she was more needed here, and came and pressed her warm body against Joe. Before long Joe could hear Prince barking again, far away.

When would someone understand what the dogs were trying to say? After a while Joe no longer heard Prince. A deep silence fell over the wooded hill.

Joe must have dozed a little. Uncomfortable as he was, he was very tired, too, and the warmth of the dogs and the sense of their friendliness had made him relax somewhat.

Out of this shallow sleep he suddenly awoke to the sound of voices calling his name through the woods, and of people talking to each other some distance apart so that they had to shout. Betsy and Shaggy barked, and Joe raised his head and saw beams of flashlights piercing the darkness among the bare trees far away. They were coming closer moment by moment.

Joe yelled with all his might. "Here I am!" but it was not a very loud call, for the cold and pain had made him feel weak.

Prince, far ahead of the advancing people, came loping to Joe, intensely excited. He had succeeded in bringing help to his beloved Joe at last! He was beside himself.

He licked Joe's hands, dashed off and looked up the embankment toward the people, and barked and came back to Joe again.

At last the people with the flashlights neared the sloping gully's edge opposite the spot where Joe lay. Joe could recognize their voices. And in the shafts of light he glimpsed his father and three others, who turned out to be Dan, Phil and Mr. Avery.

"Joe!" Dad called. "Are you all right?"

Joe called back that he thought his leg was broken.

"Will you be all right until we find a way to get you out of there?" Mr. Avery asked. And Joe assured him that he would be.

"We'll bring you out in a minute, now," his father said. Joe could tell that he was terribly upset, but was trying not to show it.

Dan and Phil shouted to him. "You okay, Joe?" and "Hey, what happened? How'd you break your leg?"

How wonderful it was to hear all their voices.

Dan called to Betsy then, "Well, Betsy, taking care of Joe?" And Mr. Avery talked to Shaggy. The dogs got up and barked earnestly in response, and then lay down again.

177

Prince, seeing that Joe's family was well in touch with him at last, stopped barking, too, and lay down at Joe's feet to add his warmth to that of the other dogs.

Dr. Collins, Dan, Phil and Mr. Avery had reached the bottom of the embankment and in another moment were at Joe's side.

Dr. Collins knelt by Joe and put his hand on his face briefly and affectionately. "Where does your leg hurt, Son?" he asked tenderly. And Dan and the others stood by silently now.

Joe showed his father his hurt leg, but asked him not to touch it because it would just hurt more.

Dr. Collins took off his own coat and laid it over Joe carefully. A little of it lay over the dogs too, keeping them snug.

"Good dogs," said Dr. Collins gently. "You're very good dogs."

He and Mr. Avery consulted about what to do, and decided that three of them would build a fire to keep Joe warm, while Mr. Avery would drive back in his car to get Dr. Havers. Dr. Collins knew that a person with a broken leg should, if possible, not be moved until his leg was put in splints. He decided that another few minutes' wait there would be safer than carrying Joe out of the woods in his condition. Mr. Avery left immediately, and Phil followed him a little way, looking for dry wood for the fire.

178

*"Where does your leg hurt, Son?" he asked tenderly*

Joe asked for his mother. And Dan stopped to tell him, "She and Marty have gone to Jasons' to look for you, because they couldn't get them on the phone to ask." Then he asked Joe, "How did Betsy and Shaggy get out here? Did you take them along to the Jasons' this morning?"

"No," Joe said. "Prince brought them here after I fell."

"He really did?" Dan cried in amazement.

"I never thought that dogs could be quite so intelligent, and quite such devoted friends," said Dr. Collins, and he sounded deeply moved. "The way those dogs were keeping you warm, Joe, and barking for help on the road. . . . I wouldn't have believed it."

Dan ran off to join Phil in his hunt for firewood.

Now there were sounds of voices and tramping footsteps and breaking branches from the other side of the hill—in the general direction from which Joe had come hours ago. And in another moment, Mrs. Collins, Marty, Mr. Jason and Tom came walking up the gully.

"Who's there?" Mrs. Collins called out.

Dr. Collins answered; and then told her that they had found Joe. She asked quickly whether he was safe.

"Yes, Joe's safe enough now," Dr. Collins answered. "But he has a broken leg, and that doesn't feel too good. Mr. Avery has gone for Dr. Havers."

"Oh," came Mrs. Collins' distressed voice. Then as she reached Joe's side she said, "Thank heaven we've found you, dear."

And Marty said, "Oh, Joe! Gee, I was scared about you."

Dan and Phil had been off in the woods all this time, gathering branches and sticks to make a fire. And now they came back with armfuls, and dropped them near Joe.

Dr. Collins thanked the boys and examined the wood quickly to see if it were dry enough. It would do, he saw, for though some of it was wet from the rain, the dampness was only on the surface. The other pieces of wood the boys had found had been sheltered under heaps of dry leaves and would burn quickly. And there was a pile of dry leaves, too, which they had dug out from the bottom of a thick drift. These would start the fire.

Dr. Collins laid the leaves and branches in a well-built stack, and held his cigarette lighter to them. The flames leaped up in a lusty flare, and in a moment the heavier wood caught fire and began to burn steadily. The warmth spread to Joe, the fine life-restoring, encouraging warmth.

Again there were sounds of voices in the woods. It was Mr. Avery, returning with Dr. Havers. Mr. Avery was carrying the back seat of his car. They came into the gully, and Dr. Havers quickly knelt down beside Joe and examined his leg.

In another few minutes the doctor had set Joe's leg temporarily, and put it in splints so that he could be moved. He would take him to the hospital, he said, and X-ray the leg, and then, if necessary, set it better.

Dr. Collins and Mr. Avery picked Joe up, put him on the car seat, and raised it carefully at the ends, ready to carry. Mr. Jason led the way with his flashlight and Mrs. Collins and the rest came with the other lights. The dogs, still serious but much relieved, stayed close by. And so Joe was brought out of the woods.

In another hour he was comfortable in a hospital bed. Dr. Havers had set his leg properly and put it in a cast. And he was warm and snug and safe.

## CHAPTER FOURTEEN

## *Pals*

AUTUMN gave way to winter, and strong, cold winds whipped the bare trees outside Joe's windows. The sky was gray most of the time now, and there were occasional flurries of snow.

## The Right Dog for Joe

From his bed Joe watched the snowfall, and longed to be outdoors like the rest of the boys and girls of Brewster Hills. But he could not get about, for his leg was still in a cast.

But Joe was not too lonely. His own family gave him more attention, it seemed to him, than he had ever had before. And Prince not only stayed in the room with him most of the day, but was even allowed to sleep beside his bed at night. That was wonderful! Prince had been with him like this all the weeks since the fearful night in the gully. Everybody felt he belonged here, that he had first rights at Joe's side.

Joe had lots of other company, too. His friends of the neighborhood and from school came—boys and girls, and grown people.

When Dan came, he brought Betsy; and when Mr. and Mrs. Avery and Sue came, they brought Shaggy. As these two dogs had worked with Prince to save Joe, they too had a right to see how Joe was getting on, it was agreed.

Through the visitors' talk, the Collinses found out more of the details about what the dogs had done the night of Joe's accident.

A close neighbor said that Prince had appeared alone at the Collins house about seven-thirty. The neighbor knew that the Collinses were not at home, for the house was dark. So he wondered about Prince being there without Joe. And he was surprised at his barking so loudly and persistently, for he was a quiet dog, who never barked except for good reason. Still, he had not really suspected trouble. He had just wondered.

Another neighbor, Mrs. Price, said she saw Prince down at Dan's house just a little later than that. As Dan was away with his mother for the day, Betsy, his dog, was in Mrs. Price's care. Sometime after she saw Prince around the place, she called Betsy to give her her supper; and she was troubled when she found the little black and tan dog was gone. But Mrs. Price had supposed she would return when Dan got home, and so she went about her business of getting supper for her family. Now, of course, she realized what had happened. Prince had come to get help for Joe from his friend Dan; and finding him and his mother out, had somehow communicated the trouble to the Manchester-beagle, Betsy, and the two had gone off together.

Mr. Avery reported on what had happened around his place. He said that he had his first inkling that something was wrong when Shaggy disappeared. Shaggy was very much at home at their house now. She considered her small, energetic self the defender and protector of the family, and never left the grounds without one of them. So her disappearance, shortly after Mr. Avery let her outdoors for her last scamper of the evening, puzzled him greatly. Later he began to wonder about it more and more. And that eventually led him to telephone to Dr. Collins.

Another part of the story, of course, was told to Joe by his parents and his sister. Marty arrived home about nine-thirty that night. Not seeing Joe there, she went to the telephone to call the Jasons to find out why he was so late. But after some minutes of vain ringing, the operator reported that the line was out of order. That worried her, and she was glad when, a half hour or so later, her parents arrived and she could tell them everything.

Dr. and Mrs. Collins at first thought that Joe was probably quite safe. He might be delayed because he was waiting for someone who was to drive him home. Yet, since they could not reach the Jasons on the telephone to inquire, Mrs. Collins decided that she would drive out to make sure Joe was all right, and to bring him home.

Dr. Collins had a slight cold, and so agreed to let her go, so that he could get right to bed. Mrs. Collins had not yet taken off her coat and hat, and she got right back into the car; and Marty went along to keep her company.

Prince, Betsy and Shaggy must all have been with Joe in the woods, far off from the road, at the moment when Mrs. Collins and Marty passed, for they reported later that they did not hear barking or see any of the dogs along the way.

On arriving at the Jasons', Mrs. Collins and Marty were told Joe and his dog had left there almost five hours earlier. And since he had not arrived at home, they all knew now that something was seriously wrong. So Mr. Jason and Tom got into their car to help Mrs. Collins search for the boy. They hurried first to the near-by farm to phone Dr. Collins about it. But by this time only Marty's friend Dotty was at the house. She told them that Dr. Collins had asked her to stay there to take telephone messages, because he, too, had left to look for Joe. So Mrs. Collins hung up, and she and Marty, and Tom and Mr. Jason, began frantically to search roadsides and woods from their direction.

Dr. Collins had left to search, because a number of people had been telephoning the house ever since Mrs. Collins had left. They had all told of Prince's appearance around the neighborhood after dark without Joe. Some had told of his barking at the empty Collins house, as if asking for help.

Dan had phoned Mr. Avery to see if Betsy were there. And when Mr. Avery could only report that Shaggy was gone, too, both of them thought they had better go out and look for their dogs. Maybe they were with Prince, and Prince, of course, would be wherever Joe was. But why, they wondered, had Prince come for them? They had telephoned Dr. Collins. And so had Phil Carney—

he had heard some of the talk about Prince's unusual actions earlier that night.

Dr. Collins was seriously alarmed by now, and Mr. Avery offered to drive him and Dan and Phil out Jasons' way in his car so that they could all search for Joe.

They had sped along, and had gone about a mile and a half when they saw Prince trotting down the road toward them. He stopped to bark urgently, and then came closer. He stayed almost in front of the car, so that it would have been hard to pass without striking him.

They slowed down, of course, and Dr. Collins, thoroughly worried by now, called to the dog:

"Good boy, Prince! Where's Joe?"

Prince answered with louder and more frantic barking, and ran back the way he had come. They followed, and before long Prince stopped and turned in toward the rocky, wooded hill.

At that the car came to a stop, too, and the men and boys made their way quickly through the icy, dripping brush and trees. Prince led them to the gully and to Joe. And soon after, Mrs. Collins, Marty, Mr. Jason and Tom, also led by the sound of the barking, had come there from the other direction.

The whole story was told over and over in the neighborhood, and everyone knew that Prince, with Betsy's and Shaggy's help, had saved Joe's life. For the doctor said that the cold and exposure, together with the broken leg, might have been too much for Joe, had not the dogs kept him warm, and had they not brought the searchers to him that night.

But as it was, Joe was soon feeling fine, and his leg was mending well. By mid-December he was back at school.

In his free hours, he and Prince went everywhere together. Prince, being orderly and well-behaved, was never on a leash. He ran free like all the good dogs of this small town. Whenever Joe and Prince went anywhere near Mr. Healy, however, Joe always called Prince and made him stay at heel, or at least close beside him.

One cold, clear Sunday afternoon, when Joe and Prince were passing the Healys' place Joe saw Mr. Healy standing at the side of his house, enjoying the winter sunshine. Joe quickly called Prince to him, as usual.

Mr. Healy looked up. "Hello," he said in his clipped, rather severe way. And he came toward the boy.

Joe, ready for trouble, put his hand on Prince's collar to protect him.

Mr. Healy said, "Bring that dog of yours here a minute, will you?"

Joe was puzzled. Mr. Healy's voice did not sound quite as sharp and unfriendly as usual, but the boy was distrustful of him and protective of Prince, because Mr. Healy had always chased dogs away from his place.

So he stood still instead of going toward him.

Mr. Healy came on to Joe then. He stopped close before him and stood looking at him and Prince. His gray, pinched face relaxed somewhat.

"I heard about what that dog did for you," he said. "And those other dogs too—Shaggy and Betsy, I think you call them. I guess maybe I just never understood dogs. I guess they've got something to them."

Amazed at Mr. Healy's friendly interest, Joe said, "They certainly have, Mr. Healy."

"*Humpf,*" said Mr. Healy, and turned away. But he threw back over his shoulder, "Good luck to you, boy."

Joe could hardly believe his ears. He said, "Thank you!" And he and Prince went on.

Joe remembered how he had broken a window of Mr. Healy's dining room last spring, in his anger at the man's unkindness to dogs. He thought that since Mr. Healy had changed so, he, Joe, would somehow repay him for the window.

So, that night after supper, he got out his wallet. He had a little money, thanks to his summer's earnings at Sky Inn. He took out a dollar bill and put it in an envelope. He printed on it: "This is for the window I broke." But he did not feel he owed Mr. Healy that much, for he would probably still forget and be thoughtless of dogs sometimes.

When it was quite dark, Joe went over to the Healys'

*So, that night after supper, he got out his wallet*

place. He had left Prince at home so that he could not give him away. He stopped by the big elm tree out in front of the house and looked things over. The dining-room lights were on, and through the parted curtains Joe could see Mr. and Mrs. Healy at dinner.

Luck was with him; they were not likely to see him now. He went softly across the grass, tiptoed up to the front door, and slid his envelope under it. Then he hurried away on the far side of the house, ducked behind the hedge, and went home by a roundabout way through back streets.

He felt fine. A real load had been taken off his mind, now that he had paid for Mr. Healy's window. He thought, "I don't guess Mr. Healy and I will ever be real friends, but anyway we aren't enemies any more."

Joe had to work hard at school these days. In the weeks while he had been housebound with his broken leg, his father, mother and even Marty had helped him with his lessons so that he could keep up with his class. Still, things had happened at school that he had missed. He was just beginning to feel that he was fully abreast of everything again, when Christmas vacation came. And after that happy season was over, he at last began to catch up and be one with his class again.

And so the long, cold months of the winter went by, and spring came once more.

One mild Sunday, Joe, Marty, Dan, Phil, and Prince

and Betsy had been out to the Jasons' farm again. They got home about four o'clock in the afternoon. Marty went upstairs to take off her red flat shoes, which were gray with road dust. Joe went into the kitchen first, to get something to eat, for he was very hungry after the long tramp.

He heard the telephone ring, and started toward the hall to answer it. But his father, who had been in his study, was already taking the call.

Joe heard him talking over the phone.

"No, this isn't Joe Collins," he said. "This is his father. . . . A stray dog?" he asked. "By the railroad station?" And then, "Well, well!"

Joe's heart beat faster. What would his father say next? Would he let Joe go and get the stray dog? He stood by the kitchen door, tensely waiting for the next words.

His father said, "All right, we'll be right over. Yes, I'm in it too, now. After all, our collie, Prince, was a stray dog, too, you know. And where would we be without Prince?"

Joe felt himself glowing. "Dad!" he cried excitedly. "Did you . . . ? Are you . . . ?"

Dr. Collins put the receiver back in place and turned to his son. Their eyes met and both smiled. Then Dr. Collins turned briskly away.

"Come on, let's go," he said. "I guess you heard—

193

we've got work to do."

Joe asked, "Is it a little dog or a big one, Dad?"

His father put both hands in his pockets and rocked back on his heels, looking thoughtful. "Little, I guess," he said.

Joe went to the closet and took a small dog collar and leash.

"We'll take the car," Dr. Collins announced. "It's rather far to the station."

Father, Joe and Prince set out together. Joe rode in front beside Dr. Collins, and Prince had the back seat to himself. Father and Joe did not talk much as they went along, but just felt very content.

At the railroad station they got out and walked toward the baggage room.

Joe asked, "Did the man who phoned say where the dog was?"

"Yes," said Dr. Collins. "Over here on the north side."

The baggage master, a heavy-set, red-haired man with a red face, came out and greeted them. "Hello, Dr. Collins. Hello, Joe," he said. "Right over there." And he pointed to a carton against the outside wall of the baggage room.

"Poor dog!" Joe said. "He must be very scared, to hide in a box."

All three of them went to the carton and looked in, and so did Prince.

194

There were five puppies sleeping in the box! Five little mixed white and tan puppies, perhaps six weeks old, with broad heads and sturdy bodies.

"Gosh!" said Joe. "Five!" He glanced up quickly at his father, to see how he was taking it.

Dr. Collins did not look surprised. He must have known all along. He was just standing there, looking into the box, and then at Joe, and he appeared to be enjoying himself.

The baggage master was saying, "I figure someone from another town probably drove through here and dumped this box full of pups on us. A mean person it musta been. How'd he know someone would look after the young uns?"

"A person like that wouldn't care if they starved," said Joe indignantly.

Dr. Collins said, "Dogs are pretty fine to people. But some people don't give them much of a break." He took hold of one end of the box. "Give me a hand, Joe."

Joe grasped his end of the box firmly, and they started for the car. Joe still could hardly believe that his own dad could get this interested in dogs. But he had to, because it was really happening. The glow around Joe's heart was growing into a steady feeling of calm happiness. Now he and his father were real pals. They understood each other, and they had this interest in dogs together.

195

Again, Joe thought, he had to thank Prince for this. Without Prince it would never have happened.

They arranged themselves in the car, Joe sitting in back this time, with the box of puppies beside him, and Prince riding in front beside Dr. Collins. Prince was fascinated with the puppies, and as they drove home he kept turning around to look at them, and then at Joe and Dr. Collins. He was trying to find out just what his people were going to expect of him in connection with the puppies, so that he could act accordingly.

Dr. Collins said to Joe, "Well, this time you've really

196

got your hands full—with five strays all at once!"

"Yes, sir!" said Joe.

"After the way you worked out that dog show last spring," Dr. Collins went on, " and got homes for Shaggy and Patch—well, I predict you'll manage to find homes for these puppies, too." And then, in a tone that was full of laughter, he added, "Snap into it, will you? We can't keep five extra dogs forever."